SUPER EXPERT
ENVIRONMENT
QUIZ

SUPER EXPERT ENVIRONMENT QUIZ

Dilip M. Salwi

RUPA

Published by
Rupa Publications India Pvt. Ltd 2003
7/16, Ansari Road, Daryaganj
New Delhi 110002

Sales centres:

Allahabad Bengaluru Chennai
Hyderabad Jaipur Kathmandu
Kolkata Mumbai

ISBN: 978-81-291-0375-8

Fifth impression 2015

10 9 8 7 6 5

The moral right of the author has been asserted.

Typeset at Tarun Enterprises, Delhi

Printed at Rakmo Press Pvt. Ltd, New Delhi

*To
Yoga Narasimha for
his stimulating and
intellectual discussions*

Hello! Environment Quiz buffs!

Nowadays, the subject of environment has become something like weather. Everybody talks about it but nobody does anything about it! I had written '1000 Environment Quiz' more than a decade ago with the hope that it would give everybody a flavour of what it is all about and remove certain misunderstandings about it. The very fact the book has gone into several reprints speaks volumes about people's interest in the subject. But I must add that the response to the book had not been as much as I had expected then. In those days, environment was a very hot subject and the media was full of it. But today it has taken a back seat as the country has gone in for liberalisation and privatisation, though the subject is being seriously taught in schools, colleges and universities. Even graduate and post-graduate courses in the subject have been offered by several colleges and universities. Let's hope the coming young generation would not simply talk about environment but would do something concrete to save all of us from the onslaught of technology. I have revised the aforementioned book, adding some new questions here and there, and also divided it into two parts with new titles to suit the Super Quiz series that I have started. I am sure, they would go a long way in inculcating interest in environment as a life-long passion and career. All the best, quiz buffs!

Dilip M. Salwi

Acknowledgements

I am specially thankful to Dr N.R. Mankad for going through the manuscript patiently and suggesting changes, etc., on various aspects of the book. I am also thankful to the following persons and organisations for supplying me with photographs published in the book: Asok Samanta, Manager, Photo Archives, American Center, New Delhi; Gopi Menon of the USSR Information Center, New Delhi; Malti Jaikumar and Ravi Datta of the British Information Service, New Delhi; the CEDUST, New Delhi; Inter Nationes, Germany; Meteorologie Nationale, France; Imperial Chemical Industries Limited, U.K.; Kapur Farms, New Delhi; and Sunita Narain, Director, Centre for Science and Environment, New Delhi. Last but not the least I am thankful to my wife Smriti, daughter Neha and son Romel for bearing with me while I was busy revising the book.

Dilip M. Salwi

CONTENTS

I
FIRST THINGS FIRST

First Persons

1. Who was the first to draw the attention of the masses to animals through his cartoons?
   (a) Jim Davis   (b) K. Shanker Pillai
   (c) Fred Pierce   (d) Walt Disney

2. Who first proposed that a fundamental feature of the long-term trends in climate is a cycle of wobbles in the orbit of the earth?
   (a) James Croll
   (b) Milutin Milankovitch
   (c) Louis Agassiz   (d) Fridtjof Nasen

3. Who was the first to use the word 'Ecology', as far back as 1870?
   (a) Alfred Wallace   (b) Charles Darwin
   (c) Ernest Haeckel   (d) Charles Lyell

4. Who was the first to recognise the problem of water pollution?
   (a) Aristotle   (b) Pliny
   (c) Thales   (d) Hippocrates

5. Who was the first to warn that man could

alter climate by burning fossil fuels?
- (a) Syukuro Manabe
- (b) G. S. Callendar
- (c) Richard Wetherald
- (d) Roger Revelle

6. Who was the first to realise that gases in the atmosphere trap the sun's heat?
   - (a) Joseph Fourier
   - (b) Svante Arrhenius
   - (c) David Keeling
   - (d) John Dalton

7. Who was the first ruler in recorded history to order the establishment of wildlife sanctuaries?
   - (a) Akbar
   - (b) Alexander
   - (c) Ashoka
   - (d) Charles VI

8. Who was the first to discover the link between sulphur emissions from power stations and the acid content of rains?
   - (a) James Hutton
   - (b) John Delton
   - (c) Robert Angus Smith
   - (d) Henry Cavendish

9. Who was the first to establish the link between smoking and cancer?
   - (a) Richard Doll
   - (b) Francis Peyton Rous
   - (c) Malcolm Ross
   - (d) Otto Warburg

10. Who was the first to report the presence of whales in the southern seas, leading to their subsequent massacre?
    (a) Svend Foyn   (b) James Weddell
    (c) James Cook   (d) James Clark Ross

11. Who was the first to study the effects of chemical nutrients on plant growth?
    (a) Henry Cavendish   (b) Justus Liebig
    (c) Friedrich Wohler   (d) Victor Selford

12. Who was the first to point out the harmful effects of asbestos on human health?
    (a) Max Perutz   (b) Richard Synge
    (c) Irving J. Selikoff   (d) Morton Corn

First Things and Beings

13. Which living beings were the first to receive attention for their protection and conservation at an international level?
    (a) Reptiles   (b) Birds
    (c) Micro-organisms   (d) Marine creatures

14. Which is the first ruminant to be domesticated by man?
    (a) Ox   (b) Goat
    (c) Sheep   (d) Yak

15. Which is the world's first national park?
    - (a) Manu National Park
    - (b) Yellowstone National Park
    - (c) Rwenzori National Park
    - (d) Yosenmite National Park

16. Which is the first wind-driven commercial ship?
    - (a) *Dynaship*
    - (b) *Eagle*
    - (c) *Sailiner*
    - (d) *Shin Aituko Maru*

17. Which is the first mammal to be cloned in the world?
    - (a) Sheep
    - (b) Pig
    - (c) Mule
    - (d) Buffalo

18. Which part of the human body is the first to be affected by nuclear radiation?
    - (a) Bone marrow
    - (b) Liver
    - (c) Lungs
    - (d) Brain

19. Which is the first indoor pollutant of which the people became aware?
    - (a) Carbon dioxide
    - (b) Formaldehyde
    - (c) Radon
    - (d) Ozone

20. For the first time, violence erupted between Greenpeace members and French construction workers in Antarctica in 1989. What was the issue?
    - (a) Penguins' breeding around
    - (b) Whaling station

(c) Seals' breeding ground

(d) All

21. Which zoo was the first to display marine life to the public?
    (a) London Zoo
    (b) Vancouver Public Aquarium
    (c) Stuttgart Zoo
    (d) New York Aquarium

22. Which was the first building whose design was based on the structure of the royal water lily?
    (a) Eiffel Tower
    (b) Crystal Palace
    (c) Liverpool Railway Station
    (d) National Library of Paris

23. Which was the first animal to be domesticated by man?
    (a) Cat   (b) Dog
    (c) Horse   (d) Sheep

24. Which is the first national park to be established in India?
    (a) Velvadar National Park
    (b) Periyar National Park
    (c) Bandipur National Park
    (d) Corbett National Park

25. Who first practised fish farming in freshwater ponds?
    (a) The Chinese   (b) The Mexicans
    (c) The Polish   (d) The Romans

First Places

26. Where did the Greenpeace warriors first protest against the misuse of environment and made their presence felt?
    (a) Mururora Atoll   (b) Aleutian Islands
    (c) North Sea   (d) Orkney Islands

27. Where is the world's first permanent underground disposal site for nuclear waste located?
    (a) Near Stockholm   (b) Near Dublin
    (c) Near San Francisco (d) Near Los Angeles

28. Where did the elected representatives of various nations meet for the first time to examine the subject of environment?
    (a) Bonn, Germany   (b) London, UK
    (c) Vienna, Austria   (d) New York, USA

29. Where was geothermal energy first used to generate electricity?
    (a) Mexico   (b) Japan
    (c) Italy   (d) Russia

30. Where was photochemical smog first noticed in the world?
    (a) Los Angeles   (b) London
    (c) Paris   (d) Tokyo

31. Which city was the first to introduce quarantine laws to protect its inhabitants from diseases brought in by foreign traders?
    (a) London   (b) Paris
    (c) Venice   (d) Baghdad

32. Where was the first pilot-scale ocean thermal energy plant setup?
    (a) Off the Cuban coast
    (b) Off the Irish coast
    (c) Off Male island
    (d) Off Hawaii island

33. Which country was the first to adopt alcohol-based petrol as a fuel for its automobiles?
    (a) Austria   (b) Indonesia
    (c) Brazil   (d) Australia

34. Where was the world's first public zoo established?
    (a) Boston, USA   (b) London, UK
    (c) Paris, France   (d) Portsmouth, UK

35. Which country was the first to go for Debt-for Nature swap to protect its endangered rainforest?

(a) Zambia   (b) Madagascar
(c) Bolivia   (d) Peru

36. Where was the world's first nationwide Green party founded?
    (a) Sweden   (b) Denmark
    (c) New Zealand   (d) Germany

II

ECOLOGY

Biological Networks

37. The word 'Ecology' is derived from two Greek words. What do they mean?
    (a) The study of wild
    (b) The study of land
    (c) The study of animals
    (d) The study of home

38. Which types of plants and animals are more sensitive to over-exploitation than others?
    (a) The ones with longer life span.
    (b) The ones which breed faster.
    (c) The ones with longer life-span and which breed slowly.
    (d) The ones with shorter life-span and which breeds fast.

39. What plays a vital role in maintaining life in stored seeds?
    (a) Moisture   (b) Temperature
    (c) Pressure   (d) Radiation

40. What kind of relationship often exists between plants and fungi?

(a) Commensal   (b) Parasitic
(c) Mutualistic   (d) None

41. What is the boundary of transition between two or more communities, sharply defined or integrated, called?
(a) Epilimnion   (b) Biome
(c) Anticline   (d) Ecotone

42. What do bacteria break down dead and decaying plant and animal matter into?
(a) Humus
(b) Inorganic chemicals
(c) Elements   (d) Soil

43. What is lost when one organism consumes another?
(a) Food   (b) Water
(c) Energy   (d) Chemicals

44. Which organism can survive a temperature as low as −75 degree Celsius?
(a) Polar Bears   (b) Seeds
(c) Eggs of Penguins (d) Arctic Seals

45. What relationship exists between an Egret and a Rhinoceros?
(a) Mutualistic   (b) Commensal
(c) Parasitic   (d) None

46. Most organisms are active in a temperature

range. What is it?
- (a) 0 to 40 degree Celsius
- (b) 10 to 20 degree Celsius
- (c) 20 to 60 degree Celsius
- (d) – 5 to 25 degree Celsius

47. What kind of relationship exists between a Remora fish or Shark-sucker, and a Shark?
- (a) Commensal
- (b) Parasitic
- (c) Mutualistic
- (d) All

Chemical Networks

48. Which gas is both harmful and beneficial to life on the earth?
- (a) Oxygen
- (b) Ozone
- (c) Carbon dioxide
- (d) Methane

49. Where lies the highest concentration of 'ferro-manganese nodules' or 'manganese nodules'?
- (a) South Atlantic
- (b) North Pacific
- (c) North Indian Ocean
- (d) North Atlantic

50. When organisms die, which is the element released in several forms by bacteria?
- (a) Potassium
- (b) Sulphur
- (c) Iron
- (d) Sodium

51. Guano deposits, the excrements of sea birds

and bats, are the major source of one element.
Which one?
(a) Phosphorus   (b) Sulphur
(c) Zinc   (d) Nitrogen

52. Free oxygen is toxic to one organism. Which
one?
(a) Lichen   (b) Fungi
(c) Aerobic bacteria (d) Anaerobic bacteria

53. Which volatile substance guide insects to
crops?
(a) Progesterones   (b) Pheromones
(c) Hormones   (d) Oestrogens

54. Which is the acid associated with soil?
(a) Humic acid   (b) Acetic acid
(c) Nitric acid   (d) Sulphuric acid

55. If a species of plant contains selenium, what
does the soil in which it has grown contain?
(a) Iron   (b) Copper
(c) Silver   (d) Uranium

56. Burning of fossil fuels drastically affects a
nature's cycle. Which one?
(a) Nitrogen cycle
(b) Phosphorus cycle
(c) Carbon dioxide cycle
(d) Water cycle

57. What causes the distinct smell of sea?
    (a) Sodium chloride
    (b) Hydrogen sulphide
    (c) Sodium phosphate
    (d) Dimethyl sulphide

Ecosystems

58. Which type of landscape produces heat islands?
    (a) Urban areas   (b) Coastal areas
    (c) Islands   (d) Mountain ranges

59. What affects the number of species on an island?
    (a) Vegetation   (b) Size
    (c) Location   (d) None

60. Which ecosystem is as biologically productive as a tropical rainforest?
    (a) Grasslands   (b) Shallow water areas
    (c) Coral reefs   (d) Agricultural lands

61. In the temperate ecosystem, when do the growth of plants and trees fall?
    (a) Summer   (b) Winter
    (c) Spring   (d) Autumn

62. Which ecosystem has the highest species diversity?
    (a) Chaparral   (b) Rainforest

(c) Desert   (d) Grassland

63. What are 'pastures of the sea'?
    (a) Estuaries   (b) Coastal waters
    (c) Antarctic convergence
    (d) All

64. Which type of ecosystem is biologically the least productive?
    (a) Very deep lakes   (b) Moist forests
    (c) Grasslands   (d) Coastal seas

65. What is the stability of a grassland ecosystem mainly dependent upon?
    (a) Carnivores   (b) Grazers
    (c) Both   (d) Neither

66. Which type of ecosystem acts as a seasonal home for migratory birds?
    (a) Savannahs   (b) Grasslands
    (c) Wetlands   (d) Tundras

67. What leads to natural open lands?
    (a) Insufficient rainfall
    (b) Fire
    (c) Grazing   (d) All

68. Which is the ecosystem where species diversity is the lowest?
    (a) Deciduous forest   (b) Grassland
    (c) Tundra   (d) Boreal forest

69. Into how many zones do ecologists often divide a lake?
    (a) Four major zones (b) Three major zones
    (c) Eight major zones (d) Nine major zones

70. Which type of ecosystem is biologically the most productive?
    (a) Ordinary agricultural lands
    (b) Shallow lakes
    (c) Coastal seas
    (d) Alluvial plains

71. Most deserts do not support vegetation because they do not have this. What is it?
    (a) Sufficient nutrients
    (b) A favourable temperature
    (c) Sufficient sunlight
    (d) Sufficient water

72. Which is the most recently discovered ecosystem?
    (a) Vent   (b) Tundra
    (c) Iceberg   (d) Crater

73. What constitutes a major part of Antarctic vegetation?
    (a) Shrubs   (b) Mosses
    (c) Grasses   (d) Lichens

74. What inhibits the native plant life on Antarctica from flourishing?

(a) Temperature   (b) Drought

(c) Volcanoes   (d) All

Ecoregions

75. Which place is often referred to as the 'Valley of Death'?
    - (a) Cubatao, Brazil
    - (b) Chernobyl, Russia
    - (c) Palo Alto, USA
    - (d) Nainital, India

76. Which desert is often frequented by joyriders leading to the extinction of its flora and fauna?
    - (a) California
    - (b) Sonoran
    - (c) Gobi
    - (d) Kalahari

77. Where is the 'Valley of Flowers' located?
    - (a) Garhwal Himalayas
    - (b) Hawaii
    - (c) Virunga mountains
    - (d) Taman Negara

78. Where is the worst soil erosion taking place in the world?
    - (a) Ivory coast
    - (b) Himalayan foothills
    - (c) Alps
    - (d) Usambara mountains

79. Where is the largest stretch of mangrove in the world located?

(a) Nicaragua   (b) Surinam
(c) Bangladesh   (d) Bolivia

80. Which sea is referred to as an 'Oceanic desert'?
    (a) Red Sea   (b) Sargasso Sea
    (c) Arabian Sea   (d) Sea of Japan

81. Which is the region where soil erosion from wind is maximum?
    (a) Rajasthan, India,
    (b) Baluchistan, Pakistan
    (c) Sahel, West Africa
    (d) California, USA

82. Which region is known as the 'Polygon of Drought'?
    (a) Sao Raimundo, Brazil
    (b) Rajasthan, India
    (c) California, USA
    (d) Sahel, West Africa

83. Which continent has the greatest variety of large grazing animals?
    (a) Africa   (b) South America
    (c) Australia   (d) Eurasia

84. Which region was once the 'Fertile Cresent' of the world?
    (a) Around Indo-Gangetic plains
    (b) Around Peru

(c) Around England   (d) Around Syria

85. Where was the perennial species of highly disease resistant wild corn *Zea diploperennis* found?
    (a) Brazil   (b) Canada
    (c) USA   (d) Mexico

III

ONLY ONE EARTH

Earth Itself

86. Which is the largest landmass on the earth?
    - (a) Eurasia
    - (b) Antarctica
    - (c) Australia
    - (d) North America

87. Into how many biogeographic realms is the layer of living matter on the earth divided?
    - (a) Ten
    - (b) Nine
    - (c) Eight
    - (d) Seven

88. Of the total land area of the earth covered by glaciers, how much does Antarctica contribute?
    - (a) 50 percent
    - (b) 60 percent
    - (c) 96 percent
    - (d) 70 percent

89. The earth's magnetic axis is inclined to its axis of rotation at an angle. Which one?
    - (a) 33 ⅓ degree
    - (b) 11 ½ degree
    - (c) 22 ½ degree
    - (d) 8 degree

90. Which terrestrial feature provides low albedo (reflectivity) to sunlight?

(a) Cloud cover   (b) Oceans
(c) Ice caps   (d) Forests

91. Which is the element found most abundantly in the crust of the earth?
    (a) Silicon   (b) Aluminium
    (c) Oxygen   (d) Iron

92. What is 99 percent of the crust of the earth composed of ?
    (a) 26 elements   (b) 10 elements
    (c) 5 elements   (d) 12 elements

93. What percentage of solar energy is captured by plants to energise life on the earth?
    (a) 2   (b) 0.02
    (c) 0.2   (d) 20

94. What is the crust of the earth scientifically known as?
    (a) Troposphere   (b) Noosphere
    (c) Lithosphere   (d) Asthenosphere

95. The axis of rotation of the earth is inclined at this angle with respect to the perpendicular drawn to the line joining the centres of the earth and the sun. Which one?
    (a) 23 ½ degree   (b) 12 degree
    (c) 8 degree   (d) 19 ⅓ degree

96. When did the last major warm episode occur on earth?

(a) A.D. 1000 to A.D. 1300
(b) 5000 B.C. to 2000 B.C.
(c) A.D. 1700 to A.D. 1850
(d) 3000 B.C. to 2000 B.C.

97. In which Era did today's geography begin to take shape?
(a) Precambrian Era
(b) Palaeozoic Era
(c) Mesozoic Era
(d) Cenozoic Era

98. Stromotolites, the earliest living forms known on the earth, have been found in rocks as old as this. How many years old are these rocks?
(a) 800 million years
(b) 21,500 million years
(c) 2,200 million years
(d) 3,500 million years

99. When did the Little Ice Age occur on earth?
(a) A.D. 1020 – 1280
(b) 2500 – 1000 B.C.
(c) A.D. 1650 – 1850
(d) A.D. 1580 – 1720

100. About 2.5 million years ago, which continent pair joined, allowing an influx of animals from one continent to another,

wiping out in the process many original species?
(a) South America – North Amreica
(b) Australia – South America
(c) Eurasia – Australia
(d) Eurasia – Africa

101. When is the first gene believed to have appeared in the lifeless, saline seas of the young planet earth?
(a) 4.5 billion years ago
(b) 5.0 billion years ago
(c) 4.0 billion years ago
(d) 3.5 billion years ago

102. When did flowering plants evolve on the earth?
(a) Permian period
(b) Devonian period
(c) Cretaceous period
(d) Triassic period

103. About 13,000 years ago, there existed a bridge between one pair of continents when wildlife crossed over from one to the other continent. Which one?
(a) South America – North America
(b) Australia – South America
(c) North America – Eurasia
(d) South America – Eurasia

104. Which were the first living beings to establish themselves on rocky slopes?
    - (a) Toads
    - (b) Grasses
    - (c) Lichens
    - (d) Frogs

105. When did birds evolve on earth?
    - (a) Tertiary period
    - (b) Jurassic period
    - (c) Silurian period
    - (d) Devonian period

Earth's Surface

106. Where do sinkholes occur?
    - (a) Carbonate rocks
    - (b) Sulphate rocks
    - (c) Phosphate rocks
    - (d) Rock salt

107. What is the latest period of geological time?
    - (a) Tertiary
    - (b) Devonian
    - (c) Cretaceous
    - (d) Quaternary

108. Where does 'Mohorovicic Discontinuity' occur?
    - (a) Crust and mantle
    - (b) Warm and cold ocean currents
    - (c) Mantle and core
    - (d) Warm and cold air currents

109. What takes ages to develop but only one generation of human beings to destroy?

    (a) Minerals   (b) Groundwater
    (c) Glacier   (d) Topsoil

110. What is aquifer associated with?
    (a) Water   (b) Groundwater
    (c) Rain water   (d) Sea erosion

111. Watershed is the boundary, often a ridge of high ground between two things. Which ones?
    (a) Two channels (b) Two river basins
    (c) Two streams   (d) Two lakes

112. What type of soil exists in a desert land?
    (a) Aridisols   (b) Spodosols
    (c) Alfisols   (d) Mollisols

113. Continental plates are moving with respect to each other on the surface of the earth. Which plates are moving at the greatest velocity?
    (a) South American and North American plates
    (b) Antarctic and Indo-Australian plates
    (c) Indo-Australian and Eurasian plates
    (d) Pacific and Nazca plates

114. Which feature had a dramatic and swift birth?
    (a) The Himalayas
    (b) The Mediterranean Sea

(c)   The Alps   (d)   Sri Lanka

115. What is the geological name of 'Regolith'?
(a)   Topsoil   (b)   Loam
(c)   Sand   (d)   Silt

Water

116. What percentage of water is present on the
earth in the form of seas and oceans?
(a)   80 per cent   (b)   97 per cent
(c)   90 per cent   (d)   88 per cent

117. Where is rainfall often higher than others?
(a)   Mountains   (b)   Plains
(c)   Valleys   (d)   Coastal plains

118. What causes winds and ocean currents to
follow a path deflecting to the right in the
northern hemisphere and to the left in the
southern hemisphere?
(a)   Coriolis effect
(b)   Solar tide
(c)   Ekman transport
(d)   Sea zonation

119. Ice-caps and glaciers lock up the percentage
of all freshwater available on the earth. How
much?

(a) 30 per cent   (b) 50 per cent
(c) 10 per cent   (d) 70 per cent

120. Which source of water is often misunderstood in all aspects because it is 'out of sight, out of mind'?
(a) Groundwater   (b) Clouds
(c) Snow   (d) Iceberg

121. Today, glaciers cover this percentage of the land surface of the earth. How much?
(a) 10 per cent   (b) 23 per cent
(c) 25 per cent   (d) 30 per cent

122. Which sea has two simultaneous currents moving in opposite directions?
(a) Arabian Sea   (b) Dead Sea
(c) Mediterranean Sea
(d) North Sea

123. Which mountain acts as a physical barrier to the movement of monsoon over Indian soil?
(a) Vindhyas   (b) Sahyadris
(c) Himalayas   (d) Satputra

124. What percentage of the total water present on earth is in continuous circulation?
(a) One per cent   (b) Three per cent
(c) Two per cent   (d) Zero

125. Fish and marine beings are able to survive at lower depths even when a lake is apparently frozen at the top. Why?
    (a) Water is a bad conductor of heat.
    (b) Water has a maximum density at about 4 degree Celsius.
    (c) Water has a minimum density at about 4 degree Celsius.
    (d) Water has a minimum density at about −4 degree Celsius.

Nature's Working

126. In which light does maximum photosynthetic activity in plants take place?
    (a) Red light   (b) Blue-green light
    (c) Yellow light   (d) Orange light

127. When a volcano erupts, which nature's cycle is affected?
    (a) Phosphorus cycle
    (b) Nitrogen cycle
    (c) Carbon cycle   (d) None

128. Which phenomenon causes forest fires?
    (a) Lightning   (b) Cyclone
    (c) Volcano   (d) Earthquake

129. 'Red tide' is a misnomer for a dramatic increase in the population of a particular species in sea. Which one?
    (a) Plankton   (b) Crab
    (c) Shrimp   (d) Fish

130. Which phenomenon is still a conjecture?
    (a) Greenhouse effect
    (b) Ozone holes
    (c) Global warming (d) Tsunami

131. Which natural phenomenon conducts carbon dioxide fixation in plants?
    (a) Sunlight   (b) Cosmic rays
    (c) Thunder   (d) Rain

132. What are Rossby waves related to?
    (a) Weather   (b) Seismic belt
    (c) Ocean   (d) Pond

133. Photosynthesis takes place only in those plants containing this compound. Which one?
    (a) Carotin   (b) Xanthophyll
    (c) Chlorophyll   (d) All

134. Barrier reefs are formed when some marine organisms secrete this. What is it?
    (a) Potassium-rich matter
    (b) Sulphur-rich matter

(c) Silica-rich matter

(d) Calcium-rich matter

135. Which volcanic eruption in recorded history drastically affected solar radiation and brought about major weather changes all over the earth?

(a) Mount St. Helens

(b) Kelut

(c) Krakatoa

(d) Mount Pelee

136. Which natural phenomenon is the major cause of concern among environmentalists?

(a) Avalanches   (b) Forest fires

(c) Tornadoes   (d) Ball lightning

IV

CIVILISED NEEDS

Products from Living Beings

137. Which plant is known as the gasoline plant?
     - (a) *Salvadora persica*
     - (b) *Sterculia foetida*
     - (c) *Thevetia peruviana*
     - (d) *Euphorbia lathyris*

138. What is the Alaska Fur Seal hunted mainly for?
     - (a) Fat
     - (b) Fur
     - (c) Meat
     - (d) All

139. Which tree contains a very powerful insecticide?
     - (a) Baobab
     - (b) Neem
     - (c) Kevda
     - (d) Tamarind

140. What is the Bird of Paradise mainly hunted for?
     - (a) Wings
     - (b) Tail feathers
     - (c) Meat
     - (d) Eggs

141. A laxative is obtained from the leaves of a plant native of Egypt. Which is that plant?

(a) Senna   (b) Aloe
(c) Cocoa bush   (d) Nightshade

142. What was Ostrich mainly hunted for earlier?
    (a) Meat   (b) Tail feathers
    (c) Skin   (d) Long legs

143. India is a source of this plant whose root contains a tranquiliser. Which plant?
    (a) Mayapple   (b) Curare
    (c) Henbane   (d) Rauwolfia

144. Which bird was shot in large numbers to obtain plumes for ladies hats?
    (a) Peregrine Falcon
    (b) Whooping Crane
    (c) Egret   (d) Kingfisher

145. Castor oil is obtained from castor bushes. Where were these bushes originally found?
    (a) Egypt   (b) Italy
    (c) China   (d) Nigeria

146. What were whales hunted mainly for?
    (a) Meat   (b) Teeth
    (c) Oil   (d) Bones

147. Which product is obtained from Safflower?
    (a) a cooking oil   (b) a lubricant
    (c) a hot drink   (d) a gum

148. Which virulant type of carcinogen (cancer-causing agent) is present in the mould *Aspergillus flavus* that grows on groundnuts and some grains?
    (a) Phenacetin   (b) Benzidine
    (c) Vinyl chloride (d) Aflatoxin

149. Before refrigeration came into use, what was used to preserve foodstuffs?
    (a) Pepper   (b) Cardamom
    (c) Clove   (d) Cinnamon

150. Which part of the whale is used as a perfume base?
    (a) Blubber   (b) Ambergris
    (c) Bones   (d) Teeth

151. Which is known as India's contraceptive plant?
    (a) *Mallotus philippensis*
    (b) *Helicteres isora*
    (c) *Dioscorea deltoidea*
    (d) *Terminala bellerica*

152. Which is the main agent of food-borne disease in industrialised countries?
    (a) *Campylobacter* (b) *Crytosporidium*
    (c) *Toxoplasma gondi*
    (d) *Salmonella*

153. Until recently, the importance of this component of food was ignored because it has no food value and is indigestible. Which is this component?
    (a) Minerals   (b) Water
    (c) Carbohydrates   (d) Roughage

154. Which aspect of food is the abbreviation GRAS associated with?
    (a) Hygiene   (b) Nutrition
    (c) Safety   (d) All

155. Which mineral is required in food for the proper functioning of nerves and muscles of the body?
    (a) Calcium   (b) Potassium
    (c) Chlorine   (d) All

156. Which type of food is at present a subject of controversy and debate?
    (a) Fast foods   (b) Irradiated foods
    (c) Canned foods   (d) All

157. Which mineral's absence in the food causes brittle bones and teeth?
    (a) Potassium   (b) Iodine
    (c) Calcium   (d) Phosphorus

158. Which revolution is concerned with the production of food crops?

(a) White Revolution
(b) Red Revolution
(c) Green Revolution
(d) None

159. Which source of colour additives to foods can cause cancer?
(a) Herbs   (b) Seeds
(c) Coal tar   (d) Fruits

160. Which *dal,* a common food of the poor people in India, causes Lathyrism?
(a) *Arhar*   (b) *Moong*
(c) *Chana*   (d) *Khesari*

161. Where is krill – the future food for millions –found in plenty?
(a) Around Antarctica
(b) Around Greenland
(c) Arctic Ocean
(d) North Atlantic Ocean

Energy

62. Which is the biggest energy source on the surface of the earth?
(a) Coal   (b) Tides
(c) Nucleus of atoms
(d) Solar radiation

163. As a fuel, why is charcoal preferred to wood?
    (a) Higher calorific value
    (b) Less pollution
    (c) Easy to store and transport
    (d) All

164. What percentage of solar energy received on the surface of the earth is reflected into space?
    (a) About 20 per cent
    (b) About 60 per cent
    (c) About 50 per cent
    (d) About 80 per cent

165. Which type of fuel produces a higher concentration of suspended particles when burnt in a cooking stove?
    (a) Wood   (b) Dung cakes
    (c) Twigs   (d) Crop residues

166. What is the ideal site for an Ocean Thermal Energy plant?
    (a) Near the Equator
    (b) Near the North Pole
    (c) Near any island
    (d) Near a coral reef

167. Which country has committed itself to phasing out its nuclear power stations by 2010?

(a) Canada   (b) Sweden
(c) Norway   (d) Israel

168. It is estimated that this energy striking the surface of the United States every 20 minutes is sufficient to meet the country's entire power needs for one year, if it could be harnessed. What is it?
(a) Cosmic rays   (b) Solar energy
(c) Microwave   (d) Lightning

169. Which type of house consumes the minimum amount of energy in building it?
(a) House of burnt bricks
(b) Mud house
(c) House of reinforced concrete
(d) House of cement blocks

170. Which fuel triggered off the Industrial Revolution?
(a) Oil   (b) Wood
(c) Coal   (d) Biomass

171. Which country has one-third of the world's known coal reserves?
(a) India   (b) Russia
(c) Zambia   (d) China

172. Which energy-generating source also produces a good quality of fertiliser?

(a) Thermal power plants
(b) Biogas plants
(c) Nuclear power plants
(d) None

173. Which tree has received attention in recent years as a source of fuel and food?
(a) Deodar   (b) Acacia
(c) Leucaena   (d) Lasora

174. Which country has installed the largest number of biogas plants?
(a) India   (b) Ethiopia
(c) Kenya   (d) China

175. What does conservation of energy lead to?
(a) Less expense   (b) Less pollution
(c) Conservation of resources
(d) All

Invention

176. Which invention has made it possible for us to study the entire earth and its various environments in totality?
(a) Rocket   (b) Television
(c) Satellite   (d) Computer

177. Which invention opened a window on the micro-cosmos that surround us?

(a) Binoculars   (b) Microscope
(c) Thermometer   (d) Camera

178. Which modern invention led to a faster reduction in the population of whales?
(a) Harpoon gun   (b) Submarine
(c) Explosive
(d) Steam-powered ship

179. Which invention made it possible for an individual to dive into the sea and ocean depths to explore and admire sea environment?
(a) Aqualung   (b) Bathyscape
(c) Submarine   (d) None

180. Which invention opened a window on the cosmos of which we are a part?
(a) Astrolabe   (b) Telescope
(c) Sextant   (d) All

181. Which invention mechanised farming all over the world?
(a) Tractor
(b) Irrigation pump
(c) Harvesting machine
(d) All

182. Which invention has created light pollution affecting the observation of the night sky?

(a) Electric bulb   (b) Flourescent tube
(c) Sodium lamp   (d) All

183. Which invention has become a part of a literary term representing a particular environment?
(a) Railways   (b) Electricity
(c) Jet   (d) Concrete

184. Which invention is likely to change the working and living environment of man in a big way in the near future?
(a) Space station (b) Robot
(c) Computer   (d) Satellite

185. Which invention has made the world sit on the brink of extinction?
(a) Space station (b) Nuclear bomb
(c) Rocket   (d) Robot

Industry

186. The pure, fresh water of the world's oldest Baikal lake has been polluted in recent times by partly untreated sewage and industrial effluents and partly a huge factory. What does the factory produce?
(a) Cellulose   (b) Rubber
(c) Weapons   (d) Steel

187. Which industrial chemical increases a person's chance of developing leukaemia?
    (a) PCB
    (b) Benzene
    (c) Manganese
    (d) Asbestos

188. Which industry of many tropical countries is dependent on corals?
    (a) Pearl
    (b) Lime
    (c) Tourism
    (d) Salt

189. Leakage of methyl isocyanate caused the biggest industrial disaster of the recent times. What did the industrial plant manufacture where the leakage occurred?
    (a) Fertilizer
    (b) Explosives
    (c) Pesticides
    (d) Cement

190. Which organism's case of colour change after the industrial revolution is often quoted as the most striking example of natural selection as a result of environmental change?
    (a) Spotted Ladybird
    (b) Speckled Wood
    (c) Peppered Moth
    (d) Dot Moth

191. Which item of modern fishing industry is causing unnecessary harm to marine creatures and fishes?

(a) Net   (b) Hook
(c) Line   (d) All

192. What was the cause of 'Yusho' disease which occurred in Japan in 1968 from a leak in a canning factory?
(a) PCB   (b) DBCP
(c) Formaldehyde (d) Mercury

193. Which type of industry is entering business in a big way in the West in recent years?
(a) Silviculture
(b) Solid waste management
(c) Water management
(d) Air pollution control equipment

War

194. Where did the first recorded war take place?
(a) Egypt   (b) India
(c) South America   (d) Greece

195. Which weapon has totally altered the relationship of man and his fellow beings and has affected his environment drastically?
(a) Knife   (b) Bow and arrow
(c) Gun   (d) Spear

196. What percentage of petroleum produced globally do the armed forces consume?

(a) 20   (b) 12

(c) 32   (d) 6

197. When did the first recorded instance of biological warfare occur?

(a) 600 B.C.   (b) 100 B.C.

(c) A.D.1192   (d) A.D.1927

198. Which was the first city to be destroyed by a nuclear bomb?

(a) Hiroshima   (b) Nagasaki

(c) Chernobyl   (d) None

199. What is the term 'nuclear winter' associated with?

(a) Nuclear war

(b) Nuclear disarmament

(c) Nuclear weapon race

(d) Aftermath of a nuclear holocaust

200. What is the position of the weapons industry among the major industries of the world?

(a) First   (b) Second

(c) Third   (d) Fourth

201. Which island was contaminated by germ warfare experiments during the Second World War?

(a) Island of Gruinard

(b) King William Island

(c) Bikini Island   (d) Jan Mayen Island

202. Who were the first to believe that the only
way to secure peace was to prepare for war?
(a) Sumerians   (b) Romans
(c) Arabs   (d) Mayas

203. Which war concept suggests stockpiling of
nuclear arms to maintain peace?
(a) NUTS
(b) Limited Nuclear War
(c) Non-Nuclear War
(d) MAD

204. Which herbicide was used for destroying
forests in South Vietnam during the Second
Indo-China war because troops took cover
under them?
(a) Diuron   (b) Paraquat
(c) Agent Orange   (d) Diquat

V

POLLUTION CONTROL

General

205. What is the best way to avoid the occurrence of disasters especially in factories and plants?
    (a) The people's right to know everything concerning the factories and plants and their products.
    (b) Shift factories and plants to remote regions.
    (c) Total ban on the use of their products.
    (d) Safety rules and regulations followed strictly.

206. What can control sound pollution?
    (a) Adequate urban planning and road design.
    (b) Sound-proof buildings.
    (c) Traffic control.
    (d) All

207. Air pollution can be controlled and reduced considerably, but one factor comes in its way. What is it?

(a) Politics   (b) Economics
(c) Manpower   (d) Geography

208. When lakes become acidic from acid rains, this is added to counteract the acidity. What is it ?
(a) Soil   (b) Lime
(c) Sand   (d) No solution exists

209. Which site will be most suitable for dumping non-recyclable solid but not nuclear wastes?
(a) Subduction zones
(b) Dead volcanoes
(c) Faults
(d) Rifts

210. Up to 99 per cent of cinders, fly ash and other particulate matter released during burning coal in a power station, paper mill, cement factory, etc. can be removed using a device. Which one?
(a) Electrostatic precipitators
(b) Fabric filters
(c) Bag filters   (d) All

211. What is vegetation effective in absorbing?
(a) Pollutant gases (b) Polluted water
(c) High frequency sounds
(d) All

212. If a proposal is adopted, the problem of

vehicle pollution can be brought under control in cities. Which one?
(a) Abolition of personal vehicles.
(b) Maximum use of public transport.
(c) Strict check on vehicles violating pollution limits.
(d) Planting more trees on roadsides.

213. Where do the hunters of waterfowl have to buy 'duck stamps' in the hunting season?
(a) Thailand   (b) Russia
(c) Australia   (d) North America

214. While building a landfill, what should be ensured?
(a) It is above the groundwater table.
(b) It is below the groundwater table.
(c) It is in the groundwater source.
(d) It is near a water source.

215. The pollution control programme aims to reduce the discharge of one thing into river. Which one?
(a) Oxygen-depleting waste
(b) Oxygen-producing waste
(c) Carbon-producing waste
(d) Sulphur-producing waste

216. Which chemical extensively used in industry can be dispensed with without any loss?

(a) Soaps   (b) Artificial fertilisers
(c) Pesticides   (d) Petrol

217. What will be the cheapest way to control pollution?
   (a) Lay down rules and regulations and ensure that they are implemented.
   (b) Charge polluters for the mess they make.
   (c) Distribute pollution-cleaning devices.
   (d) All.

218. How do anti-noise systems reduce repetitive noise?
   (a) By using ultrasound waves.
   (b) By using infrasound waves.
   (c) By canceling the noise waves.
   (d) By modifying the noise waves.

Daily Life

219. How would one control pollution as an individual in the present world?
   (a) Control, if not stop, consumption of industrial products.
   (b) Vote for the political candidate who supports the conservation cause.
   (c) Study the local environmental law and bring the defaulter to the notice of the authorities.

(d) Join the local environment club.

220. Which frequently used product should be bought of the plain and traditional variety?
    (a) Soap   (b) Hair shampoo
    (c) Deodorant   (d) All

221. Which is the simplest and least polluting way of supplying energy to the home?
    (a) Wind energy   (b) Solar energy
    (c) Hydroelectric energy
    (d) Nuclear energy

222. Which household chemical can be dispensed with?
    (a) Soap   (b) Shampoo
    (c) Air-freshener   (d) Disinfectant

223. Which is the most economic and pollution-free form of transport?
    (a) Solar car   (b) Electric vehicle
    (c) Bicycle   (d) Hovercraft

224. While buying foodstuff, what should be preferred?
    (a) Organically grown food
    (b) Hydroponically grown food
    (c) Canned food
    (d) Food grown on artificial fertiliser

225. Which household chemical should not be

allowed to enter the drainage system directly?

(a) Oil (b) Oil-based products
(c) Soap water (d) Washing powder

226. What is the way to prevent or reduce plastic pollution?
(a) Banning the use of plastic
(b) Using biogradable plastic
(c) Plastic recycling
(d) All

227. If one is using liquid detergents for washing purposes, one should use as small amount of it as possible or try to use one free of, or low in this. What is it?
(a) Potassium (b) Phosphate
(c) Nitrate (d) Chlorate

228. What can reduce indoor air pollution?
(a) Coal fire (b) Stove
(c) Gas flame (d) None

229. How would one fight against pollution and waste as an individual in the present world?
(a) By writing letters of protest against. polluting individuals and industries to widely read newspapers and magazines.
(b) By volunteering to participate in cleaning up a polluted place.

(c) By voting for an environment-conscious politician.

(d) All

Recycling and Waste

230. Which household waste has an excellent recycling potential?
     (a) Organic matter (b) Paper and card
     (c) Glass   (d) Metal

231. What is the useful material left in a sugarcane after its juice has been extracted?
     (a) Bagasse   (b) Dextran
     (c) Lignin   (d) All

232. Solid waste has been used in the formation of this. What is it?
     (a) Bridges   (b) Artificial reefs
     (c) Islands   (d) Reservoirs

233. Which chemical process is used to recover valuable materials from solid waste?
     (a) Hydrolysis   (b) Tanning
     (c) Slaking   (d) Pyrolysis

234. Which state of the USA passed a 'Bottle bill', a way to recycle glass, in 1972 that required all drink containers to carry a deposit and so to be returned?

(a) Montana   (b) Oregon
(c) Wisconsin   (d) Georgia

235. Which type of waste is produced in the maximum amount in a household?
(a) Paper and card (b) Plastics
(c) Metal   (d) Organic

236. Where is the world's largest household waste incinerator located?
(a) Paris   (b) Delhi
(c) New York   (d) Los Angeles

237. Which household waste does not decompose at all?
(a) Aluminium   (b) Glass
(c) Plastic   (d) All

238. Waste is unavoidable, but what is the way to minimise it?
(a) Buying products with minimum packaging materials.
(b) Reducing the consumption of products.
(c) Buying locally produced products.
(d) Buying fresh products.

239. Which country generates more municipal waste per head than any other country?
(a) Germany   (b) Japan
(c) Australia   (d) USA

VI

PORTRAIT QUIZ

240. This bearded person wrote extensively on his encounters with wild animals. What is more, he also set up a unique zoo of endangered animals. Who is he?

241. Who is this elderly, spectacled person, an extraordinary bird-watcher?

242. A staunch conservationist, this lady wrote several thought-provoking books on conservation of environment, of which the most popular is *Only One Earth*. Who is she?

243. He founded the Centre for Science and Environment in New Delhi and brought out books, monographs and a regular magazine on the state of environment in India. Who is he?

244. A crusader for animal rights in India, she has established several homes for stray animals and birds. Besides, she also writes on issues related to animals and birds.

245. He popularised the need for conserving seas, oceans and their inhabitants through his films and TV serials. Who is he?

VII

TOOLS AND TERMS

Tools

246. Which instrument is used to measure the relative humidity of air?
    (a) Hydrometer   (b) Thermometer
    (c) Micrometer   (d) Hygrometer

247. Which apparatus provides a wide variety of environmental conditions in its different chambers for the study of plants?
    (a) Greenhouse   (b) Phytotron
    (c) Test tube   (d) None

248. Which instrument is used to measure the velocity of wind?
    (a) Calorimeter   (b) Hygrometer
    (c) Anemometer   (d) Spectrophotometer

249. What does the Geiger-Muller detector detect?
    (a) Ultraviolet radiation
    (b) Infrared radiation
    (c) Nuclear radiation
    (d) None of the above

250. What are those moored or anchored objects in seas of oceans used for marking a navigational channel or obstruction or even to collect data on the surrounding environment?
    (a) Stays
    (b) Rafts
    (c) Buoys
    (d) Dhows

251. Which instrument is used to measure the turbidity of a water sample?
    (a) Flowmeter
    (b) Nephelometer
    (c) Spectrometer
    (d) Venturimeter

252. Which device is used for collecting deep-water samples?
    (a) Nansen bottle
    (b) Purse seine
    (c) Buoy
    (d) All

253. Which instrument is used for measuring minute changes in gravitational force?
    (a) Gyroscope
    (b) Gravimeter
    (c) Pendulum
    (d) Foucault pendulum

254. Which type of satellite can give an early warning of natural disasters?
    (a) Meteorological satellite
    (b) Remote-sensing satellite
    (c) Early-warning satellite
    (d) Infrared satellite

255. Which instrument is used for measuring the velocity of water?
   (a) Watermeter   (b) Flowmeter
   (c) Venturimeter   (d) All

256. What does a Tensiometer measure?
   (a) Soil cohesion
   (b) Surface tension
   (c) Soil moisture
   (d) Soil erosion

Techniques

257. Which mathematical subject is often used as a tool in environmental studies?
   (a) Trigonometry   (b) Topology
   (c) Geometry   (d) Statistics

258. Which technique is used for analysing from the earth some special atmospheres such as those of planets and their satellites?
   (a) Laser remote sensing
   (b) Mass spectroscopy
   (c) Radar
   (d) Infrared emission spectroscopy

259. Which technique can map the concentration of sulphur dioxide over a whole town by operating a gadget from one location?

(a) LIDAR

(b) Spectrophotometry

(c) Gas chromatography

(d) Mass spectroscopy

260. What is the level where physiological reactions of human workers or test animals begin to be observed called?

(a) Lethal level (b) Threshold level

(c) Limiting level (d) Toxic level

261. What is used to determine the various metal elements in soils or rocks?

(a) Ion chromatography

(b) Atomic absorption spectroscopy

(c) Infrared emission spectroscopy

(d) All

262. Toxicity is commonly measured by the exposed animals killed. How much?

(a) 25 per cent

(b) 75 per cent

(c) 50 percent

(d) 20 percent

263. Which technique is used at sea to detect and determine the position of underwater objects and also sea-depths?

(a) SONAR (b) SOFAR

(c) LORAN (d) RADAR

264. What is the standard scale used for measuring velocities of winds?
    (a) Beaufort scale (b) Richter scale
    (c) Celsius scale   (d) None

265. What do foresters examine to estimate the age of a tree?
    (a) Veins of leaves (b) Annular rings
    (c) Length of roots (d) Density of roots

Subjects

266. Under which subject does the activity of tracing serial pathways of minute organisms for various scientific and practical purposes come?
    (a) Remote sensing
    (b) Aerobiology
    (c) Environmental engineering
    (d) Aerodynamics

267. Which subject deals with the creation of new processes for utilising farm-produced materials?
    (a) Chemofarming (b) Organic farming
    (c) Chemurgy
    (d) Agricultural chemistry

268. What is the study of the effects of natural

environment on living organisms called?
(a) Bioclimatology
(b) Biometeorology
(c) Climatopathology
(d) Climatophysiology

269. Which aspect of disease does epidemiology deal with?
(a) Causative agents
(b) Disease carriers
(c) Societal
(d) Mass transmission

270. What is the study of trees as individuals in relation to their environment known as?
(a) Forest ecology
(b) Forest autecology
(c) Forest synecology
(d) All

271. Demography is the statistical study of this. What is it?
(a) Human societies
(b) Human populations
(c) Human settlements
(d) Human life

272. Which branch of ecology has mathematics and mathematical concepts as its foundation?

(a) Autecology   (b) Systems ecology
(c) Synecology   (d) Genecology

273. What is the study of lakes, ponds, rivers, streams, swamps and reservoirs which make up the inland water systems called?
(a) Hydrogeology (b) Hydrology
(c) Ecology   (d) Limnology

274. Which subject deals with the possible environmental influences on the development of species, especially of man?
(a) Paleobioclimatology
(b) Bioclimatology
(c) Biometeorology
(d) Biogeography

275. The domain of hydrology embraces the full life history of one of the following on earth. What is it?
(a) Carbon dioxide (b) Water
(c) Nitrogen   (d) Soil

276. Which branch of meteorology deals exclusively with the interaction between atmosphere and ground?
(a) Micrometeorology
(b) Aerology
(c) Weather dynamics
(d) Climatology

277. Which subject is concerned with the distribution of animals and how their past distributions has produced the present pattern?
(a) Biogeography (b) Zoogeography
(c) Zoochory   (d) All

278. Which subject deals with the relationships :between human groups and the plant species they utilise?
(a) Ecology   (b) Iconography
(c) Ethnobotany   (d) Horticulture

279. Bioacoustics is the study of this. What is it?
(a) Wildlife sounds
(b) Human sounds
(c) Acoustics of zoos
(d) Sounds in nature

280. Which subject deals with the distribution of different races of mankind?
(a) Ethnology   (b) Ethnography
(c) Ethology   (d) Epistemology

281. What is analysing the detailed chemistry and molecular structures of nature's most complex materials and using them as models for new biotechnologies called?
(a) Bioinformatics (b) Biomimicry

(c) Ecodesign   (d) Ecoengineering

282. Which of the following is an emerging subject in environmental sciences?
    (a) Geology
    (b) Geophysics
    (c) Geography
    (d) Geoinformatics

283. Which is presently a controversial subject in the field of genetic engineering?
    (a) Stem cell research
    (b) Gene therapy
    (c) Genetically modified food
    (d) All

Terms - Daily Life

284. What is 'Eco-development'?
    (a) Development of an ecosystem.
    (b) Development in tune with the health of the planetary ecosystem.
    (c) Ecosystem of a developed region.
    (d) Development in tune with an ecosystem.

285. What is 'Eco-freeze'?
    (a) Halting ecological degradation.
    (b) Stopping ecological disasters.

(c) Planning an ecological balance.

(d) Stopping the manufacture of environment-modification weapons.

286. What is 'Ecological wisdom'?
  (a) It is wise to change our life-style.
  (b) Ecological balance must be maintained at any cost.
  (c) Human beings are a part of nature, not its owners.
  (d) Greening the earth should be given the topmost priority.

287. What is 'Strangelove ocean'?
  (a) The primeval ocean.
  (b) The lifeless ocean after, say, a nuclear holocaust.
  (c) The ocean after the melting of polar ice.
  (d) The remnant ocean following an Ice Age.

288. What is 'Quality of life'?
  (a) Leading a balanced, healthy and knowledgeable life.
  (b) Leading a happy life.
  (c) Leading a life in tune with nature.
  (d) Leading a life free from tensions and stresses.

289. What is 'Voluntary simplicity'?

(a) To avoid mass consumerism.
(b) Try to lead a simple life.
(c) Not to be greedy about possessing things.
(d) All.

290. What is 'Environmental ethics'?
(a) The ethics taken into account while discussing environmental issue.
(b) Individuals, corporations and governments should handle environmental matters from ethics point of view.
(c) Environmental aspects are taken into account while tackling any ethical question.
(d) Individuals, corporations and governments assume responsibility to look into the likely consequences of their actions and activities and prevent any adverse results from deliberate or ill-considered actions.

291. What are rare species of plants, birds and animals?
(a) Those with small world population.
(b) Those threatened with extinction.
(c) Those on the verge of extinction.

(d) Those whose survival is unlikely.

292. What is a 'Green belt'?
    (a) The forest preserved to offset the pollution created in cities.
    (b) The area of semi-rural, low density population.
    (c) The belt of trees lining roads.
    (d) The forest at the outskirts of a city or town.

293. What are of rows of trees and plants raised specially to combat desiccating and eroding effects of winds on crop and rangelands known as?
    (a) Tree belts   (b) Shelter belts
    (c) Greenfield sites (d) Greenways

294. What does the term 'Overkill' deal with?
    (a) Pesticidal poisoning
    (b) Soil erosion
    (c) Nuclear holocaust
    (d) Global warming

295. What is the chemical substance or physical agent capable of inducing inheritable genetic change called?
    (a) Carcinogen   (b) Mutagen
    (c) Teratogen   (d) Tumorogen

Terms - Ecological Parlance

296. What are 'Hot spots'?
    (a) Volcanoes on the earth.
    (b) Estimated centres of volcanic activity beneath crustal plates.
    (c) Earthquake centers.
    (d) All.

297. Which living beings are not 'Consumers'?
    (a) Human beings (b) Plants
    (c) Animals   (d) Birds

298. What are 'Benthos'?
    (a) Plants and animals living at the bottom of a sea or lake.
    (b) Plants and animals living in the continental shelf.
    (c) Plants and animals living in an atoll.
    (d) Plants and animals living on the surface of a sea or lake.

299. 'Timberline' is the line on the Northern hemisphere beyond which one organism ceases to grow. Which one ?
    (a) Lichen   (b) Sedge
    (c) Tree   (d) None

300. What are 'Bio-monitors'?

(a) The animals that can be used to monitor.
(b) The plants that can be used to monitor.
(c) The non-living things that can be used to monitor pollutants.
(d) All.

301. Which term literally means being at the table together?
(a) Mutualism   (b) Parasitism
(c) Commensalism (d) All

302. What is 'Ecosystem'?
(a) A self-sustaining community of plants and animals taken together with its inorganic environment.
(b) A community of plants and animals along with their environment.
(c) A system which is in an ecologically balanced state.
(d) A system with the potential for ecological balance.

303. What is 'Mulch'?
(a) Dead plants.
(b) Dead trees.
(c) Dead plant material that accumulates on the ground.
(d) Dead animals that decay and merge with the soil.

304. What is 'Biochemical Oxygen Demand'?
    (a) The amount of oxygen consumed in decomposing inorganic wastes.
    (b) The amount of oxygen consumed in decomposing inorganic and organic wastes.
    (c) The amount of oxygen consumed in decomposing organic wastes.
    (d) The amount of oxygen consumed in decomposing plants.

305. Which living beings are 'Tertiary consumers'?
    (a) Plants.
    (b) Micro-organisms.
    (c) Meat-eating animals.
    (d) Plant-eating animals.

306. What is 'Gene pool'?
    (a) All the genes and their different alleles in a population of a plant or animal species
    (b) All the genes of a plant or animal species
    (c) All the genes of a plant or animal species pooled at one place
    (d) Genes pooled together in an organism

307. What is 'Mutation'?
    (a) Genetic correction

(b) Genetic mistake

(c) Genetic pathway

(d) Genetic line

308. Which environmental assessment term deals exclusively with the carbon content of an environment?

(a) BOD   (b) COD

(c) TOC   (d) POC

Terms - Technical

309. Which term represents the sum total of life on earth?

(a) Biomass   (b) Gaia

(c) Biosphere   (d) Biome

310. What is the major migration pathway used by the waterfowl known as?

(a) Flyover   (b) Flyway

(c) Flyroute   (d) Flyby

311. What is the fine residue suspended in exhaust gases due to incomplete combustion known as?

(a) Pollutant   (b) Plume

(c) Dust   (d) Fly ash

312. What is any living thing that successfully competes with people for food, space, or

other essential needs called?

(a) Virus   (b) Bug
(c) Parasite   (d) Pest

313. What is the largest terrestrial community that can be easily recognised by a biologist called?
    (a) Pioneer community
    (b) Biomass
    (c) Biosphere
    (d) Biome

314. What does the acronym 'POP' stand for?
    (a) Popular Organic Pesticides
    (b) Persistent Organic Pollutants
    (c) Purified Organic Products
    (d) Prime Organic Products

315. What are herbicides, aviacides, algacides, rodenticides, fumigants, etc, called?
    (a) Biocides   (b) Pesticides
    (c) Insecticides   (d) Fungicides

316. What is a random change in the distribution of genes in a population as the number of individuals in the population decreases known as?
    (a) Genetic erosion
    (b) Gene jumping
    (c) Genetic drift
    (d) Mutation

317. What is the dominance of a new genetic form as a result of environmental change called?
   (a) Adaptation   (b) Natural selection
   (c) Succession   (d) Synergism

318. What is the ability of a population to grow in an unrestricted environment where no forces work to slow the growth rate called?
   (a) Carrying capacity
   (b) Biotic potential
   (c) Biomass conversion
   (d) Lead time

319. What is the marine life that migrated to the Red Sea or Mediterranean, when the Suez Canal was opened, known ecologically as?
   (a) Lessepsian migrants
   (b) Suezian migrants
   (c) Ferdinandian migrants
   (d) No special name has been given

320. What is a junk of appliances and vehicles known as?
   (a) Garbage   (b) Trash
   (c) Solid waste   (d) Rubbish

VIII

HISTORY, FAILURES AND SUCCESSES

History

321. Which ancient people built huge aqueducts that brought water from distant sources?
    (a) Romans   (b) Harappans
    (c) Incas   (d) Sumerians

322. Which element is believed to be responsible for the decline of the Roman Empire because it affected the mental capacity of the Romans?
    (a) Lead   (b) Mercury
    (c) Arsenic   (d) Nickel

323. Which animal's total extermination helped the White man bring the Red Indian to his knees?
    (a) Bison   (b) Beaver
    (c) Mink   (d) Rabbit

324. The entire demand of the Roman Empire for this grain was met by what are today the

sandy, African shores of the Mediterranean. Which is it?

(a) Barley   (b) Rice

(c) Wheat   (d) Maize

325. What is the main ecological factor that led to the collapse of the Mayan civilisation around A.D.900?

(a) Flood   (b) Soil erosion

(c) Avalanches   (d) Pollution

326. Which ancient civilisation has an ordinance passed to protect people from noise due to metal works and keeping roosters?

(a) Indian   (b) Greek

(c) Chinese   (d) Babylonian

327. Which European King ordered that a man should be tortured for burning coal and fouling the air?

(a) King George I   (b) Charles V

(c) Louis XIV   (d) King Edward I

328. What is the main ecological factor that led to the fall of the Sumerian civilisation around 2000 B.C.?

(a) Soil erosion   (b) Salination of soil

(c) Flood   (d) All

329. Which ancient empire had huge arenas for

witnessing fights between men and hungry
animals?

(a) Gupta Empire (b) Roman Empire
(c) Aztec Empire (d) Mughal Empire

330. Where did people carve huge statues known
today the world over for their magnificence
but in the process invited an ecological
disaster?

(a) Cook's Island (b) Easter Island
(c) Madagascar (d) Hawaii

Disasters

331. Which highly toxic compound was released
into the atmosphere when an explosion
occurred at a chemical factory at Seveso,
Italy?

(a) Aldrin   (b) Dieldrin
(c) Chlorinated hydrocarbon
(d) Dioxin

332. What was the cause of the Irish potato
famine of the late 1840s when two million
people died and another two million became
refugees?

(a) Failure of monsoon
(b) Monoculture

(c) Floods.
(d) Genetic erosion

333. Which dam killed several hundreds of people by flooding that occurred when huge rocks slid into it?
(a) Vaiont Dam, Italy
(b) Mangla Dam, Pakistan
(c) Hoover Dam, USA
(d) Hirakud Dam, India

334. What caused the Chernobyl disaster?
(a) Nuclear test
(b) Nuclear reactor accident
(c) Nuclear waste disposal leak
(d) Nuclear weapon accident

335. A pesticide poison exported from Germany to kill sugarcane rats in Guyana affected a large population of that country, and even caused deaths. Which is that pesticide?
(a) Pyrethrin   (b) Carbaryl
(c) Phosvel   (d) Thallim sulphate

336. How did the Buffalo Creek mining disaster in 1972 that destroyed an entire village occur?
(a) When the dam holding a lake of hot coal sludge burst.
(b) When the ventilating shaft of the mine collapsed.

    (c) When water from a nearby lake flooded the mines and the neighbouring region.

    (d) When a fire set off an explosion in the mines.

337. What does the name *Amoco Cadiz* go down in history for?
    (a) Nuclear waste site
    (b) Oil slick
    (c) Toxic cloud
    (d) Forest fire

338. What is the famous 'Love Canal' incident concerned with?
    (a) Chemical plant accident
    (b) River pollution
    (c) Toxic waste dump
    (d) Man-made bacteria

Expeditions and Projects

339. In 1500 B.C. Queen Hatshepsut of Egypt sent an expedition to a country to look for the frankincense tree. Where was the expedition sent?
    (a) Africa   (b) India
    (c) China   (d) Europe

340. Which explorer of plants brought the plant

producing the drug curare from the Amazon basin to Europe?

(a) Richard Gill
(b) Richard Spruce
(c) Hugh A. Weddell
(d) Joseph Jussieu

341. Which plant explorer identified centres of extreme genetic diversity?

(a) Joseph Banks   (b) William Hooker
(c) Joseph Hooker (d) N.I. Vavilov

342. Which expedition was devoted to the study of all the aspects of an entire ocean?

(a) HMS Challenger Expedition
(b) German Atlantic Expedition
(c) Meteor Research Expedition
(d) None

343. For which commodity did Christopher Columbus want to cross the Atlantic and reach India?

(a) Spices   (b) Cassava
(c) Maize   (d) Gold

344. Which project was designed to determine the ability of humans to live at relatively great depths for long periods?

(a) Alvin   (b) Piccard
(c) Sealab   (d) Beebe

345. The conservation and protection of a bird was the mission of Project Grus. Which one?
    (a) Common Crane
    (b) Siberian Crane
    (c) Blacknecked Crane
    (d) Sarus Crane

IX

ESTABLISHMENTS

Organisations

346. Where is the World Resources Institute located?
    (a) Singapore
    (b) Washington DC
    (c) Brisbane
    (d) Los Angeles

347. Which newspaper regularly publishes the 'Survey of the Environment' containing features and reports on various aspects of environment in India?
    (a) *The Deccan Herald*
    (b) *The Hindustan Times*
    (c) *The Hindu*
    (d) *The Telegraph*

348. Where are the headquarters of the International Union for the Conservation of Nature and Natural Resources located?
    (a) Paris   (b) Melboune
    (c) Ottawa   (d) Gland

349. Where is the Centre for International Environmental Information located?
    (a) Melbourne   (b) New York
    (c) Bonn   (d) Frankfurt

350. Which organisation campaigns for the protection of species?
    (a) Earthscan   (b) Club of Earth
    (c) Club of Rome   (d) Earthwatch

351. Which organisation brought out *Looking Back to Think Ahead GREEN India 2047* containing up-to-date information on various aspects of environment and new strategies for growth and development?
    (a) Tata Energy Research Institute
    (b) Centre for Science and Environment
    (c) Energy and Environment Group
    (d) Indian Institute of Ecology and Environment

352. Where is the office of Scientific Committee on Problems of the Environment located?
    (a) Nairobi   (b) Paris
    (c) Gland   (d) London

353. Where are the headquarters of the World Commission on Environment and Development located?
    (a) Geneva   (b) London

(c) Cairo   (d) Melbourne

354. Where is the International Register of Potentially Toxic Chemicals located?
    (a) New Delhi
    (b) Pairs
    (c) Washington DC
    (d) Geneva

355. Where are the headquarters of the 'Friends of the Earth' located?
    (a) New York   (b) Oslo
    (c) London   (d) Auckland

356. Where is the Smithsonian Institution Center for Short-Lived Phenomena located?
    (a) Massachusetts (b) Victoria
    (c) Trinidad   (d) Florida

357. Which organisation plans to bring out 'Traditional Knowledge Digital Library' containing botanical and medical information from ancient Indian sources?
    (a) NISCAIR   (b) TERI
    (c) CSE   (d) NISD

358. Where is the International Council of Environmental Law located?
    (a) Tokyo   (b) Bonn
    (c) London   (d) Bangkok

359. Where are the headquarters of the United Nations Environment Program located?
 (a) Rome (b) Washington DC
 (c) Nairobi (d) Mumbai

360. Which world body brings out the *World Conservation Strategy*?
 (a) I.U.C.N. (b) W.W.F-N
 (c) U.N. (d) Earthlife

361. Where is the International Institute for Environment and Development located?
 (a) Gland (b) London
 (c) Montreal (d) New Delhi

362. Where is the International Crane Foundation located?
 (a) Wisconsin (b) Bharatpur
 (c) Tokyo (d) Montreal

Institutions: Local

363. Where is the Indian Institute of Forest Management located?
 (a) Shimla (b) Mysore
 (c) Karaikudi (d) Bhopal

364. Where is the Pollution Control Research Institute located?
 (a) Karad (b) Burla

(c) Jabalpur   (d) Haridwar

365. Where is the Indian Grassland and Fodder Research Institute located?
(a) Patna   (b) Palampur
(c) Bhubaneswar (d) Jhansi

366. Where is the Central Soil and Water Conservation Research Centre located?
(a) Kolhapur   (b) Bhubaneswar
(c) Jaipur   (d) Dehradun

367. Where is the National Institute of Occupational Health located?
(a) Bokaro   (b) Ahmedabad
(c) Visakhapatnam (d) Udaipur

368. Where is the Industrial Toxicological Research Centre located?
(a) Lucknow   (b) Hyderabad
(c) Tripura   (d) Dibrugarh

369. Where are the headquarters of the National Bureau of Plant Genetic Resources located?
(a) Shimla   (b) New Delhi
(c) Jodhpur   (d) Bangalore

370. Where is the Centre for Environmental Education located?
(a) Pune   (b) Ahmedabad
(c) Cochin   (d) Guwahati

X

BOOKS

Books

371. Which book links spirituality with environmental awareness and conservation?
    (a) *The Awakening Earth*
    (b) *Green Inheritance*
    (c) *Good Work*
    (d) *Abandon Affluence*

372. When was Thomas Malthus's essay on the 'Principle of Populations as It Affects the Future Improvement of Society' published?
    (a) 1852   (b) 1683
    (c) 1798   (d) 1903

373. Which book lists the endangered species of flora and fauna of the world?
    (a) *Club of Rome Report*
    (b) *State of the Ark*
    (c) *The Sinking Ark*
    (d) *Red Data Book*

374. Which book is subtitled *Economics as Though People Mattered*?

(a) *Small is Beautiful*
(b) *The Energy Fix*
(c) *The Real Cost*
(d) *Abandon Affluence*

375. Which best-selling novel is concerned with a fight between an engineer and environmentalists over the building of a thermal power station?
(a) *Overload*   (b) *Dogs of War*
(c) *Cheaspeake*   (d) *Congo*

376. When did Rachel Carson's book *Silent Spring* produce worldwide awareness about nature conservation and environment?
(a) 1950   (b) 1971
(c) 1962   (d) 1942

377. Which organisation brings out the *Red Data Book*?
(a) I.U.C.N.   (b) WWF-N
(c) UNEP   (d) ICBP

378. What is 'Our Common Future'?
(a) The Greens' Manifesto
(b) CITES report
(c) IUCN report
(d) The Brundtland report

379. When was the important book *Limits to Growth* published?

(a) 1958   (b) 1982

(c) 1964   (d) 1972

380. What is Kai Curry-Lindahl's excellent book *Let Them Live* about?
    (a) Elephants
    (b) Tigers
    (c) Cheetah
    (d) All near extinct beings

381. Which book talks in detail about the effects of a nuclear holocaust?
    (a) *The Fate of the Earth*
    (b) *Ill Fares the Land*
    (c) *Battle for the Planet*
    (d) *The First Three Minutes*

Authors

382. Who wrote the controversial book. *The Skeptical Environmentalist* which bases all environmental arguments on statistics and mathematics?
    (a) Anil Agarwal
    (b) Bjorn Lomberg
    (c) Chandiprasad Bhatt
    (d) Petra Kelly

383. Who wrote the book *The Web of Life* on the

multi-disciplinary networks about human development and future of life on earth?

(a) Jim Lovelock (b) Hazel Henderson
(c) Fritjof Capra (d) Lester Brown

384. Who wrote *Architecture for the Poor* focusing on designing houses using mud?

(a) Laurie Baker (b) Hasan Fathy
(c) Francis D. Hole (d) All

385. Who wrote *The Water Manifesto-Arguments for a World Water Contract* opposing the privatisation of water and turning it into a commodity?

(a) Vandana Shiva
(b) Riccardo Petrella
(c) Kenneth Boulding
(d) E. O.Wilson

386. Who wrote *Small is Beautiful* which advocated the use of a technology in tune with the environment?

(a) Freeman Dyson
(b) E.F. Schumacher
(c) Andy Porter
(d) M.K. Gandhi

387. Who wrote the bestseller *Gorillas in the Mist* describing the lives of mountain gorillas?

(a) George B. Schaller

(b) Dian Fossey
(c) Richard Leakey
(d) Jane Goodall

388. Who wrote the best-selling book *The Fate of the Earth*?
(a) Frank Barnaby
(b) Des Wilson
(c) Carl Sagan
(d) Jonathan Schell

389. Who wrote the autobiographical book *My Pride and Joy*?
(a) George Adamson
(b) Norman Myers
(c) Jane Goodall
(d) Julian Huxley

390. Who wrote *Since Silent Spring*, a sequel to the classic which brought awareness of environment the world over?
(a) James Watts
(b) Rene Dubos
(c) Jeremy Cherfas
(d) Frank Graham Jr

391. Who is the author of *The First Eden*, the book that gives the environmental history of lands the surround the Mediterranean Sea?
(a) Andrew Neal

    (b) Susan George

    (c) John McCormick

    (d) David Attenborough

392. Who wrote the widely acclaimed book *Tiger! Tiger!*?

    (a) Kailash Sankhala

    (b) Valmik Thapar

    (c) Arjun Singh

    (d) Ramesh Bedi

393. Who wrote the book *Temples or Tombs*? concerning controversies centred on environment versus industry?

    (a) Anil Aggarwal (b) T. Shivaji Rao

    (c) Madhav Gadgil (d) Darryl D' Monte

394. Who wrote the book *The Sinking Ark* on the fast-depleting resources of the earth?

    (a) Gerald Durrell (b) David Bellamy

    (c) David Lee (d) Catherine Caufield

395. Who authored the classic *Lifetide* dealing with life and its biological rhythms?

    (a) Lewis Thomas

    (b) Carl Sagan

    (c) Lyall Watson

    (d) David Attenborough

XI

DATES

Important Dates

396. Which year of the Earth Summit is considered to be a milestone in awakening the world to the need for working together for sake of the planet?
     (a) 1972   (b) 1982
     (c) 1992   (d) 2002

397. When was the Project Elephant set up by the Ministry of Environment and Forests Government of India?
     (a) 1979-80   (b) 1884-85
     (c) 1991-92   (d) 1995-96

398. When did the International Human Genome Consortium announce the complete decodification of instructions that govern how humans develop and function?
     (a) 2002   (b) 2001
     (c) 2003   (d) 2000

399. When was the Botanic Gardens Conservation Secretariat set up to expand the role of

botanic gardens in conserving threatened species?

(a) 1962   (b) 1985
(c) 1973   (d) 1971

400. When was the International Whaling Commission meant to regulate whale catches and to protect endangered species established?

(a) 1952   (b) 1928
(c) 1932   (d) 1946

401. Which decade has been declared the International Decade for Natural Disasters Reduction?

(a) 1980 to 1989 (b) 1990 to 1999
(c) 2000 to 2009 (d) 2010 to 2019

402. When was the Tropical Ocean Global Atmosphere Programme started?

(a) 1980   (b) 1985
(c) 1975   (d) 1970

403. When did the Three Mile Island Nuclear Reactor disaster occur?

(a) 1972   (b) 1979
(c) 1980   (d) 1976

404. When was the Royal Society for the Protection of Birds founded?

(a) 1871   (b) 1889
(c) 1820   (d) 1921

405. In which year was the first Earth Day celebrated in the United States?
(a) 1962   (b) 1957
(c) 1975   (d) 1970

Turning Points

406. When was the 'Man and the Biosphere', a broad-based ecological programme, launched by the UNESCO?
(a) 1967   (b) 1971
(c) 1983   (d) 1953

407. When was Greenpeace founded?
(a) 1952   (b) 1963
(c) 1969   (d) 1981

408. When did the World Bank, which loans money for development projects, set up an environment department?
(a) 1962   (b) 1972
(c) 1982   (d) 1987

409. When did the UN Conference on the Human Environment present the notion of 'Ecodevelopment'?

(a) 1972 (b) 1982
(c) 1962 (d) 1952

410. When was the World Wide Fund for Nature started?
(a) 1972 (b) 1961
(c) 1975 (d) 1960

411. When was the International Union for Conservation of Nature and Natural Resources set up?
(a) 1950 (b) 1957
(c) 1948 (d) 1962

412. Which year is known as the International Geophysical Year when a massive effort was made to study the earth and its atmosphere?
(a) 1986 (b) 1957
(c) 1962 (d) 1973

413. When was the United Nations Environmental Programme started?
(a) 1942 (b) 1963
(c) 1972 (d) 1981

414. In which year was the Clear Air Act put into operation in London, when thousands died of suffocation from smoke?
(a) 1952 (b) 1956
(c) 1922 (d) 1982

415. When was the World Conservation Strategy launched?
    (a) 5 June 1981
    (b) 6 March 1980
    (c) 9 January 1978
    (d) 20 July 1960

416. When did the U.S. Supreme Court rule that man-made organisms, in particular Ananda Chakrabarti's 'Superbug' to clean oil spills, can be patented under existing laws?
    (a) 1976   (b) 1978
    (c) 1980   (d) 1984

XII

CULTURE

Religion

417. Which Indian religious sect has commandments prohibiting felling of green trees and killing of animals?
    (a) Shaivaites   (b) Arya Samajists
    (c) Vaishnavas   (d) Bishnois

418. Which plant's cultivation was banned in 1519 in Mexico because it was closely associated with religious ceremonies of the Aztecs?
    (a) Dioscorea   (b) Rubber
    (c) Potato   (d) Amaranth

419. How would the following passage from the Bible be described in modern ecological terms: 'And the fish that was in the river died; and the river stank, and the Egyptians could not drink of the water of the river; and there was blood through out all the land of Egypt'?
    (a) River eutrophication
    (b) Nuclear waste site

(c) River pollution

(d) None of the above

420. Who is considered the patron saint of ecology?
(a) Gautama Buddha
(b) St. Francis
(c) Tukaram
(d) Sai Baba

421. Which tree is famous as the 'Bodhi tree' or 'Tree of Enlightenment'?
(a) Peepal   (b) Ashoka
(c) Tulip Tree   (d) Devil's tree

422. Which religious community welcomes the vultures that come to dispose of the dead?
(a) Sikhs   (b) Hindus
(c) Parsees   (d) Jews

423. Which religious book contains the ecologically correct phrase, 'All flesh is grass'?
(a) the *Koran*
(b) the *Vedas*
(c) The *Bible*
(d) the *Granth Sahib*

424. Which religious book gives a lot of information on how horses should be cared for and how they should be bred?

(a) the *Bible*   (b) the *Upanishads*
(c) the *Talmud*   (d) the *Koran*

425. Who said, 'The desert is the Garden of Allah, from which the Lord of the Faithful removed all superfluous human and animal life, so that there might be one place where he can walk in peace'?
  (a) Omar Khayyam (b) Rumi
  (c) Averroes   (d) Anonymous

426. Which Hindu code urges man to protect plants and animals for his own survival and prosperity?
  (a) *Manu Smriti*   (b) *Yagnyavalka Smiti*
  (c) *Dharmasastra* (d) All

427. Which type of monkey is held in veneration, almost taken as an incarnation of a God, by the Hindus?
  (a) Leaf Monkey   (b) Common Langur
  (c) Golden Langur (d) Rhesus Macaque

Language and Art

428. Which element is associated with the phrase 'mad as a hatter'?
  (a) Arsenic   (b) Cadmium
  (c) Mercury   (d) Chromium

429. When a single piece of evidence is not enough to prove anything, this migratory bird is referred to. Which is it?
(a) Wagtail   (b) Flamingo
(c) Rosy Starling (d) Swallow

430. 'Everybody talks about the weather, but nobody does anything about it '.Who said this?
(a) William Wordsworth
(b) William Shakespeare
(c) Walt Whitman
(d) Charles Dudley Warner

431. What does the natural phenomenon 'El Nino' mean?
(a) Little boy   (b) Big boy
(c) Little mother   (d) Little brother

432. Nothing or no one is perfect. In order to say this, the characteristic of one common sight is evoked. Which one?
(a) Garden   (b) Pond
(c) Tree   (d) Road

433. Which animal and its spots are referred to when it is to be said that a man cannot change his character?
(a) Fishing cat (b) Cheetah
(c) Leopard   (d) Snow Leopard

434. When things appear gloomy, this phenomenon of nature is referred to inspire hope. What is it?
(a) Rainbow　　　(b) Rain
(c) Cloud　　　　(d) Sunrise

435. When human beings of similar taste come together, their behaviour is compared with that of this being. Which one?
(a) Frogs　　　　(b) Birds
(c) Monkeys　　　(d) Lions

436. Which painter's celebrated painting 'Progress' showed a balanced reconciliation of nature and culture, way back in 1853?
(a) Cezanne
(b) Delacroix
(c) Asher B. Durand
(d) Edouard Manet

437. Who created the cartoonstrip hero Pogo with a programme to clean up pollution and with a slogan, 'We have met the enemy and he is us!'?
(a) Malcolm Hancock
(b) R. Palazzo
(c) Ajit Ninan Mathew
(d) Walt Kelly

438. Which Indian artist of the past drew a portrait of the extinct bird Dodo?

(a) Manu Lal   (b) Mirza Sangi Beg
(c) Ustad Mansur   (d) Vishnu Prasad

439. Who is considered to be the pioneer realistic painter of landscapes?
(a) Claude Lorrain   (b) Alexender Cozens
(c) Claude Monet   (d) Gustave Courbet

440. Which Indian King of the British Raj collected drawings of Indian plants, animals, birds, etc., made by Indian artists?
(a) Raja Serfoji of Tanjore
(b) Raja Ram Singh of Jaipur
(c) Raja Sayajirao Gaekwad of Baroda
(d) Raja Ranjit Singh of Patiala

Myths and Symbols

441. Which extinct bird has become the symbol of extinction?
(a) Mountain Quail
(b) Dodo
(c) Pinkheaded Duck
(d) Forest-spotted Owlet

442. Which flower is the cradle of the universe in Hindu mythology?
(a) Marigold   (b) Rose
(c) Indian Lotus   (d) Chrysanthemum

443. Where did the myth of a fire-breathing dragon prevail in ancient times?
(a) China   (b) Hawaii
(c) Peru   (d) Egypt

444. Which was considered the home of the mythical bird Phoenix?
(a) China   (b) Arabia
(c) Peru   (d) Scotland

445. Which people's legend contains the story of the 'Warriors of the Rainbow' who would restore the earth to her former beauty?
(a) Mayans   (b) Red Indians
(c) Vikings   (d) Maoris

446. According to Indian mythology, all the plants are created from the hair of this God. Which one?
(a) Brahma   (b) Vishnu
(c) Indra   (d) Maheshwar

447. Which bird has represented imperial power for millennia?
(a) Falcon   (b) Vulture
(c) Lammergeier (d) Eagle

448. Which animal is the symbol of the World Wide Fund for Nature?
(a) Red Panda   (b) Polar Bear
(c) Tiger   (d) Giant Panda

449. Which animal is commonly depicted as a symbol of fertility in many ancient religions of the world?
    (a) Cat   (b) Bull
    (c) Dog   (d) Fox

450. Which bird is the national symbol of the USA?
    (a) Peregrine Falcon
    (b) Bald Eagle
    (c) Rock Pigeon
    (d) Green Heron

451. Which bird is the symbol of the Bombay Natural History Society?
    (a) Hornbill   (b) Egret
    (c) Spoonbill   (d) Sunbird

XIII

INDIAN SCENARIO

General and Topical

452. Which body gives the Rajiv Gandhi Wildlife Conservation Award for making an impact on the protection and conservation of wildlife in India?
    (a) Department of Science and Technology
    (b) Ministry of Environment and Forests
    (c) Centre for Science and Environment
    (d) National Natural History Museum

453. Which Indian scientist recently received the International Volvo Prize for his contributions to environmental studies?
    (a) Madhav Gadgil (b) S.Z.Qasim
    (b) Aditi Pant   (d) R.K.Singh

454. Which Indian literary figure recently wrote an essay and pamphlet in support of the 'Narmada Andolan' after studying the entire case in details?
    (a) Vikram Seth   (b) Ruskin Bond
    (c) Arundhati Roy   (d) Arun Joshi

455. Which Indian literary figure wrote *Countdown* describing the reality of a nuclear war between India and Pakistan?
   (a) Amitav Ghose
   (b) Vikram Seth
   (c) Namita Gokhale
   (d) Arundhati Roy

456. A type of soft drink came under fire in India due to high levels of this chemical. What is it?
   (a) Pesticide
   (b) Colouring agent
   (c) Artificial sweetener
   (d) All

457. Who spearheads the 'Narmada Andolan' (movement) in India?
   (a) Medha Patkar
   (b) Rajinder Singh
   (c) M.C.Mehta
   (d) Sunita Narain

Places

458. In which metropolitan Indian city polluted air hangs above like a cloud?
   (a) Mumbai   (b) Kolkata
   (c) Delhi   (d) Chennai

459. Which Indian city is the first to adopt CNG (Compressed Natural Gas) for public transport?
(a) Mumbai   (b) Bangalore
(c) Delhi   (d) Chandigarh

460. This small town has the highest incidence of TB because it is a major power-loom and *bidi* centre. Which is that town?
(a) Ropar, Punjab
(b) Burhanpur, M.P.
(c) Dhule, Maharashtra
(d) Banda, U.P.

461. In which Indian city is human waste recycled for fish farming?
(a) Shillong   (b) Kolkata
(c) Visakhapatnam (d) Mumbai

462. Tuberculosis and respiratory ailments are the biggest killers in one Indian city. Which one?
(a) Nagpur   (b) Dehradun
(c) Mumbai   (d) New Delhi

463. Where did a group of environmentalists start picketing some shops selling rayon as a symbolic protest against the allocation of land to rayon industries meant for growing eucalyptus?

(a) Kanpur   (b) Calicut
(c) Nagpur   (d) Ranebennur

464. Which Indian city has the highest concentration of heavy petrochemical industries on its outskirts?
(a) Mumbai   (b) Vadodara
(c) Kanpur   (d) Gawahati

465. Where was the first biosphere reserve in India set up?
(a) Nokrek   (b) Manas
(c) Gulf of Mannar (d) Nilgiri

Wildlife

466. Which Indian bat is the largest in size?
(a) Indian False Vampire
(b) Painted Bat
(c) Flying Fox
(d) Tickell's Bat

467. Which animal that lives on trees uses its tail to climb?
(a) Toddy Cat   (b) Red Panda
(c) Binturong   (d) Leopard Cat

468. Which animal is fast disappearing from India?
(a) Cheetah   (b) Wolf
(c) Leopard   (d) Gaur

469. Where is the Snow leopard found?
    (a) Ladakh   (b) Himachal Pradesh
    (c) Sikkim   (d) Arunachal Pradesh

470. Where are man-eating tigers most commonly found?
    (a) Sunderbans   (b) Kumaon
    (c) Melghat   (d) Kanha

471. Where is the last home of the Brow-antlered Deer located?
    (a) Keibul Lamjao National Park
    (b) Kanha National Park
    (c) Corbett National Park
    (d) Keoladeo National Park

Parks

472. Which Indian bird sanctuary is essentially the hinterland of a saline lagoon?
    (a) Keoladeo   (b) Ranganathittu
    (c) Point Calimere (d) Sultanpur

473. Which Indian National Park is a vast region of mangrove swamp?
    (a) Manas   (b) Melghat
    (c) Sunderbans   (d) Indravati

474. Where is the gene sanctuary for citrus and other plants located?

(a) Nilgiri Biosphere reserve

(b) Sunderbans

(c) Garo hills

(d) Gulf of Mannar

475. Where is the Nalabana Bird Sanctuary located?

(a) Sultanpur lake

(b) Dal lake

(c) Chilka lake

(d) Silsit lake

476. Which park floats in a vast lake?

(a) Velvadar National Park

(b) Keibul Lamjao National Park

(c) Keoladeo National Park

(d) Madhupur National Park

477. Where is the Padmaja Naidu Himalayan Zoological Park, which houses and breeds a number of endangered and rare species of wildlife, located?

(a) Srinagar (b) Haridwar

(c) Darjeeling (d) Gangtok

Crusaders

478. Who founded 'Pani (water) Panchayats' and transformed villages in some parts of India?

(a) Rajinder Singh
(b) Vilasrao Salunkhe
(c) Sundarlar Bahuguna
(d) Ela Bhatt

479. Who stood unsuccessfully for the 1989 Parliament election with the sole aim to promote the cause of environment?
(a) Maneka Gandhi
(b) Z.R. Ansari
(c) Chandiprasad Bhatt
(d) Shivram Karanth

480. Which Indian army wing has taken up the task of preserving and restoring the ecology of the country?
(a) Border Security Force
(b) Central Reserve Police Force
(c) Territorial Army
(d) None

481. Which politician of pre-Independent India was an ornithologist?
(a) Annie Besent
(b) Allan Octavian Hume
(c) Jawarharlal Nehru
(d) Bal Gangadhar Tilak

482. Who was the first to suggest the setting up of environmental courts in the country to

deal exclusively with crimes relating to environment?

(a) V.R. Krishna Iyer

(b) Maneka Gandhi

(c) Soli Sorabji

(d) P.N. Bhagwati

483. Which body advises the Indian Government and industry on how to maintain a healthier and cleaner environment in the country as well as develop it economically?

(a) NCEPC (b) NCSTC

(c) NEERI (d) NMNH

XIV

LAST THINGS

Quotes and Records

484. Who said, 'The tiger is only an index of environmental quality'?
    (a) Peter Scott
    (b) Ramesh Bedi
    (c) Kailash Sankhala
    (d) George Schaller.

485. Whose famous words are: 'In wilderness is the preservation of the world'?
    (a) Henry David Thoreau
    (b) Ralph Waldo Emerson
    (c) Gifford Pinchot
    (d) Petra Kelly

486. Who said, 'We abuse land because we regard it as a commodity belonging to us. When we see land as a community to which we belong, we may begin to use it with love and respect'?
    (a) Julian Huxley (b) Aldo Leopold
    (c) Norman Myers (d) Lester R. Brown

487. Which astronaut remarked, 'The vast loneliness of the Moon... makes you realize just what you have back there on earth...'?
   (a) Yuri Gagarin (b) John Glenn
   (c) Jim Lovell (d) Frank Borman

488. Who said, 'In nature there is enough for everyone's need, but too little for everyone's greed'?
   (a) Lewis Mumford
   (b) Thomas Mann
   (c) Barry Commoner
   (d) M.K. Gandhi

489. Who said, 'Conservation in its widest sense brings a peace of mind which is very difficult to define — Just walking under trees, among greenery gives you something that you cannot get anywhere else'?
   (a) Salim Ali (b) Dave Foreman
   (c) Rachel Carson (d) Mariam Rothschild

490. Who said, 'The shadow of the future space ship, indeed, is already falling over our spend thrift merriment'?
   (a) Kenneth E. Boulding
   (b) Vandana Shiva
   (c) Ivan Illich
   (d) E. O.Wilson

491. Who said, 'Forests are mothers of rivers'?
    (a) Sunderlal Bahuguna
    (b) Arnold Toynbee
    (c) Jacob Bronowski
    (d) Charles Darwin

492. Who said, 'The environmental movement has got to re-educate people'?
    (a) Margaret Mead (b) J.B.S. Haldane
    (c) Anita Roddick (d) Edward Teller

493. Who said, 'Evolution is a creative process, in precisely the same sense in which composing a poem or a symphony, carving a statue...(and) painting a picture are creative acts'?
    (a) Theodosius Dobzhansky
    (b) Fritjof Capra
    (c) Jacob Bronowski
    (d) Rene Dubos

494. Who said, 'Ecology is permanent economy'?
    (a) Sunderlal Bahuguna
    (b) Rachel Carson
    (c) Rene Dubos   (d) Barbara Wald

495. Who said, 'Now there is one outstandingly important fact regarding Spaceship Earth, and that is that no instruction book came with it'?

(a) Otto Frankel

(b) R. Buckminster Fuller

(c) Arthur C. Clarke

(d) Gerald Durrell

496. Who said, 'We shall never understand the natural environment until we see it as a living organism'?
(a) Paul Ehrlich (b) Margaret Mead
(c) Erich Fromm (d) Paul Brooks

497. Who said, 'The environment is everything that isn't me'?
(a) Bertrand Russell
(b) A.N.Whitehead
(c) Karl Popper
(d) Albert Einstein

498. Who said 'We won't have a society if we destroy the environment'?
(a) Margaret Mead (b) Erich Fromm
(c) E.O.Wilson (d) Peter F. Drucker

499. Which is the world's worst case of a monument corroded by air pollution?
(a) Taj Mahal, India
(b) Cologne Cathedral, Germany
(c) Acropolis, Italy
(d) Cleopatra's Needle, USA

500. Which is the largest tiger reserve in India?
   (a) Indravati   (b) Simlipal
   (c) Dudhwa   (d) Nagarjunasagar

501. Which country has the world's richest diversity of birds?
   (a) India   (b) Myanmar
   (c) Colombia   (d) Zaire

502. Which city in the world has the highest sulphur dioxide pollution?
   (a) Milan   (b) Seoul
   (c) New Delhi   (d) Rio de Janeiro

503. Which is the world's longest glacier?
   (a) Malaspina Glacier
   (b) Lambert Glacier
   (c) Pindari Glacier
   (d) Frederikshaab Glacier

504. Where is the biggest cavern located?
   (a) Sri Lanka   (b) China
   (c) Australia   (d) Indonesia

505. Which is the world's saltiest lake?
   (a) Red Sea   (b) Arabian Sea
   (c) Dead Sea   (d) China Sea

506. Which is the world's largest bay?
   (a) Wailvis Bay   (b) Bay of Bengal
   (c) Mossel Bay   (d) San Francisco Bay

507. Which is the largest flowering plant?
     (a) Chinese wisteria
     (b) Rafflesia
     (c) Sunflower
     (d) Lotus

XV

MISCELLANY

508. Which day has been declared as 'World Coconut Day' to make people aware of its vital role in reducing poverty and providing nutrition?

   (a) June 5   (b) September 2
   (c) February 28   (d) October 20

509. Which warrior asked his troops to obtain drinking water by desalinating sea water?

   (a) Julius Caesar   (b) Shivaji
   (c) Akbar   (d) George Patton

510. Which vehicle is considered to be an 'All Terrain Vehicle' (ATV)?

   (a) Truck   (b) Jeep
   (c) Bus   (d) Car

511. If Antarctica were to melt, by how much would the level of seas rise?

   (a) About 100 metres
   (b) About 60 metres
   (c) About 160 metres

(d) About 10 metres

512. Antarctica is an uncontaminated and well preserved source of this. What is it?
(a) Diamonds   (b) Krill
(c) Meteorites   (d) Crystals

513. Which heavenly body is likely to hit the earth in the coming years and create unprecedented damage on its surface?
(a) Apollo Object (b) Kuiper Object
(c) Asteroid   (d) Trojan

XVI

PHOTO QUIZ

514. This seems to be a scene from Disney Land - something to do with fun. But, it is really a serious affair. What is it? What does it do?

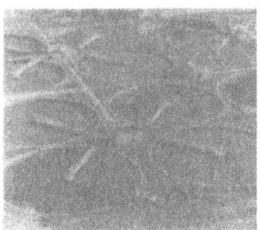

515. What are these tall trees? What is special about them?

516. Anything special about this highway? Yes, there is something special. What is it? What is its purpose?

517. What is this strange-looking device for? Identify it and its use.

518. What is the metallic arm? What is its purpose? What is being watched on the TV screen?

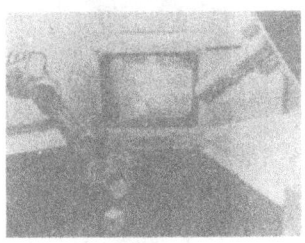

519. What kind of vehicle is this person handling? What is its purpose? Where will it be used?

520. This is an artist's impression of a plant. What is it? Where will it be installed and what use will it be put to?

521. This device is floating on the surface of the sea. What is its purpose?

522. Clouds right on the ground? What else could they be? What are they meant for?

523. What are these vessels? What are they supposed to do?

524. What are these dots surrounding the earth?

525. A novel type of house built for the first time in India. What is so special about it?

ANSWERS

1. (d)
2. (a) Milankovitch refined it further using mathematics.
3. (c)   4. (d)   5. (b)   6. (a)
7. (c)   8. (c)   9. (a)   10. (c)
11. (b)   12. (c)   13. (b)

14. (b) and (c) Controversial, in some regions sheep, others goat.
15. (b)   16. (d)   17. (a)   18. (a)
19. (b)   20. (a)   21. (a)   22. (b)
23. (b)   24. (d)   25. (a)
26. (b) To prevent a nuclear test.
27. (a)   28. (a)   29. (c)   30. (a)
31. (c)   32. (a)   33. (c)   34. (c)
35. (c)   36. (c)   37. (d)
38. (c) For example, whales and large tropical hardwood trees.
39. (a) and (b)   40. (b)   41. (d)
42. (a)   43. (c)   44. (b)   45. (d)
46. (a)   47. (a)
48. (b) At ground level, harms life; in the atmosphere shields life from harmful radiations.
49. (b)   50. (b)   51. (a)   52. (d)
53. (b)   54. (a)   55. (d)   56. (c)

57. (d) Released by algae.
58. (a)   59. (b)   60. (c)   61. (b)
62. (b)   63. (b)   64. (a)   65. (b)
66. (c)   67. (d)   68. (c)
69. (b) Littoral, Limnetic and Profundal.
70. (d)   71. (d)
72. (a)Volcanic sites and rifts on the ocean floor.
73. (d)   74. (b)
75. (a) Worst pollution exists there.
76. (a)   77. (a)   78. (b)
79. (c) Sunderbans; some part of it is in India.
80. (b)   81. (c)   82. (a)   83. (a)
84. (d)   85. (d)   86. (a)
87. (c) Nearctic, Palaearctic, Neotropical, Indomalayan, Africotropical, Oceanian, Australian, and Antarctic.
88. (c)   89. (b)   90. (d)   91. (c)
92. (b)   93. (b)   94. (c)   95. (a)
96. (a)
97. (c) To be precise, the late Mesozoic Era.
98. (d)   99. (c)   100. (a)   101. (d)
102. (c) To be precise, the early Cretaceous period.
103. (c) Now Berring Strait.   104. (c)
105. (b)   106. (a)   107. (d)   108. (a)
109. (d)   110. (b)   111. (b)   112. (a)
113. (d)   114. (b)   As little as one century.
115. (a)   116. (b)   117. (a)   118. (a)
119. (d)   120. (a)   121. (a)   122. (c)

123. (c)   124. (a)   125. (b)
126. (a) and (b) 127. (a)   128.(a) and (c)
129. (a)   130. (c)   131. (a)   132. (a)
133. (c)   134. (d)   135. (c)   136. (b)
137. (d)   138. (b)   139. (b)   140. (b)
141. (a)
142. (b) Not any more but nowadays it is hunted for its (c) skin – for making handbags.
143. (d)   144. (c)   145. (a)   146. (c)
147. (a)   148. (d)   149. (c)   150. (b)
151. (c) Contains a number of steroid drugs.
152. (d)   153. (d)
154. (c) Generally Recognised As Safe.
155. (d)   156. (b)   157. (c) and (d)
158. (c)   159. (c)   160. (d)   161. (a)
162. (d) Exceeds the sum of other sources by 5,000.
163. (d)   164. (d)   165. (b)   166. (a)
167. (b)   168. (b)   169. (b)   170. (c)
171. (d)   172. (b)   173. (c)   174. (d)
175. (d)   176. (c)   177. (b)
178. (a) and (d)   179. (a)   180. (b)
181. (d)   182. (d) All street lights.
183. (d) Concrete jungle.   184. (c)
185. (b)   186. (a)   187. (b)   188. (b)
189. (c)   190. (c)
191. (a) Made of synthetic material, it is rot-proof and strong and can become a hazard to

marine beings if carelessly thrown into the sea.

192. (a)
193. (b)
194. (a) Occurred in 3200 B.C. between upper and lower Egypt.
195. (c)   196. (d)
197. (a) The Athenian legislator Solon poisoned the water supply in the city of Kirrha with the noxious roots of the plant 'Helleborus'.
198. (a)   199. (d)
200. (b) Second only to oil industry.
201. (a) Part of Scotland.
202. (c)
203. (d) Mutually Assured Destruction.
204. (c)   205. (a)   206. (d)
207. (b) Pollution controlling equipment are highly expensive presently.
208. (b)   209. (a)   210. (a)   211. (c)
212. All
213. (d) Revenue thus generated is used in improving and preserving waterfowl habitats.
214. (a)   215. (a)
216. (b) Modern chemical industries thrive on the propaganda that artificial fertilisers increase food production. Actually they cause considerable health and environmental problems.
217. (b)   218. (c)   219. (a)

220. (a) and (b) Useless additional ingredients create more pollution.
221. (b)
222. (c) It pollutes the air further.
223. (c) Good for health too.
224. (a) Unfortunately, they are expensive and are scarcely available in India.
225. (a) and (b) because they form a thin film over the surface of water and harm living beings.
226. (b)
227. (b) Causes water eutrophication.
228. (a) It sets up powerful convection currents which lift pollutants out of the house through the chimney.
229. (d)   230. (a) and (b)
231. (a)   232. (b) 233. (d)   234. (b)
235. (a) and (d)
236. (a)   237. (c) 238. (a)   239. (d)
240. Gerald Durrell   241. Salim Ali.
242. Barbara Ward.   243. Anil Agarwal.
244. Maneka Gandhi.
245. Jacques Yues-Cousteau.
246. (d)   247. (b) 248. (c)   249. (c)
250. (c)   251. (b) 252. (a)   253. (b)
254. (b)   255. (b) and (c)
256. (c)   257. (d) 258. (d)   259. (a)
260. (b)   261. (b) 262. (c)   263. (a)

264. (a)   265. (b) 266. (b) 267. (c)
268. (a)   269. (d) 270. (b) 271. (b)
272. (b)   273. (d) 274. (a) 275. (b)
276. (a)   277. (b) 278. (c) 279. (a)
280. (b)
281. (b) and (c)
282. (d)   283. (d)
284. (b) and (d)
285. (a)   286. (c) 287. (b)
288. (a) Nowa days, (c) and (d) also define this.
289. (d)   290. (d) 291. (a) 292. (b)
293. (b)
294. (c) With the available nuclear weapons, the earth can be destroyed several times.
295. (b)   296. (b) 297. (b) 298. (a)
299. (c)   300. (b) 301. (c) 302. (a)
303. (c)   304. (c)
305. (c) A carnivore eating another carnivore.
306. (a)   307. (b)
308. (c) Total Organic Carbon and (d) Particulate Organic Carbon.
309. (c)   310. (b) 311. (d) 312. (d)
313. (d)   314. (b)
315. (a) Pesticide is a general term.
316. (c)   317. (b) 318. (b) 319. (a)
320. (c)   321. (a) 322. (a) 323. (a)
324. (c)   325. (b) 326. (b) 327. (d)
328. (b)   329. (b)

330. (b) Forests were cleared to plant gardens and to obtain logs for canoes and for erecting statues, which led to soil erosion, starvation, internecine wars, and cannibalism.
331. (d)   332. (b)   333. (a)   334. (b)
335. (d)   336. (a)
337. (b) 'Amoco Cadiz' is the name of the tanker which causes the oil spill off the coast of Brittany in 1978.
338. (c)   339. (a)   340. (a)   341. (d)
342. (b)   343. (a)   344. (c)   345. (a)
346. (b)   347. (c)   348. (d)   349. (b)
350. (b)   351. (a)   352. (b)   353. (a)
354. (d)   355. (c)   356. (a)
357. (a) National Institute of Science Communication and Information Resources, New Delhi.
358. (b)   359. (c)
360. (a) International Union for the Conservation of Nature and Natural Resources.
361. (b)   362. (a)   363. (d)   364. (d)
365. (d)   366. (d)   367. (b)   368. (a)
369. (b)   370. (b)
371. (a) The author is Peter Russell.
372. (c)   373. (d)   374. (a)
375. (a) The author is Arthur Hailey.
376. (c)   377. (a)   378. (d)   379. (d)
380. (d)   381. (a)   382. (b)   383. (c)

384. (b)   385. (b)   386. (b)   387. (b)
388. (d)   389. (a)   390. (d)   391. (d)
392. (a)   393. (d)   394. (c)   395. (c)
396. (c) Also called 'Rio Summit'.
397. (c)   398. (c)   399. (b)   400. (d)
401. (b)   402. (b)   403. (b)   404. (b)
405. (d)   406. (b)   407. (c)   408. (d)
409. (a)   410. (b)   411. (c)   412. (b)
413. (c)   414. (b)   415. (b)   416. (c)
417. (d)
418. (d) The Spanish leader Hernan Cortes banned its cultivation because it contains red dye used by the Aztecs in their religious ceremonies.
419. (a) The blood could be a heavy bloom of blue-green algae.
420. (b)   421. (a)   422. (c)   423. (c)
424. (d)
425. (d) An Arab saying.
426. (b)
427. (b) Also called 'Hanuman Langur' where Hanuman is the monkey God.
428. (c) The hat-makers who used to chew hat bands soaked in mercury to shape men's hats used to become temporarily intoxicated.
429. (c) One swallow does not make a summer.
430. (d)

431. (a) The phenomenon occurs around Christmas. The little boy is baby Jesus Christ.
432. (a) There is no garden without its weeds.
433. (c) The leopard cannot change its spots.
434. (c) Every cloud has a silver lining.
435. (b) Birds of a feather flock together.
436. (c)   437. (d)
438. (c) He was the court painter of Emperor Jahangir.
439. (d)
440. (a) For some time his collection was wrongly referred to as Mysore drawings.
441. (b)   442. (c)   443. (a)   444. (b)
445. (b)   446. (a)   447. (d)   448. (d)
449. (b)   450. (b)   451. (a)   452. (b)
453. (a)   454. (c)   455. (a)   456. (a)
457. (a)   458. (c)   459. (c)   460. (b)
461. (b)   462. (c)   463. (d)   464. (b)
465. (d) Set up in 1986. 466. (c)
467. (c)   468. (b)   469. (a)   470. (a)
471. (a)   472. (c)   473. (c)   474. (c)
475. (c)   476. (b) In Loktak lake, Manipur.
477. (c)   478. (b)   479. (d)   480. (c)
481. (b) Founded the Indian National Congress.
482. (d)
483. (a) National Committee on Environmental Planning and Coordination.
484. (c)   485. (a)   486. (b)   487. (c)

488. (d)   489. (d)   490. (a)   491. (a)
492. (c)   493. (a)   494. (a)   495. (b)
496. (d)   497. (d)   498. (a)   499. (c)
500. (d)   501. (c)
502. (a) Shenyang in China also falls in the same category.
503. (b)
504. (d) Sarawak Chamber in Sarawak.
505. (c)   506. (b)   507. (a)   508. (b)
509. (a)   510. (b)   511. (b)   512. (c)
513. (c)
514. A sewage treatment plant in Washington DC, USA, it releases treated water purer than the neighbouring streams.
515. Giant Sequoias which make up the famous redwood forest of California.
516. The highway is lined with transparent anti-noise shields which absorb noise and also do not affect the vision of the vehicle-drivers.
517. An energy-saving wind-driven generator which, unlike other windmills, turns around a vertical axis.
518. A robot arm being tested for exploring outer space as well as deep seas.
519. An industrial cleaning machine for use in industries to sweep floors containing hazardous materials like asbestos dust.

520. An Ocean Thermal Energy Concept which will generate electricity from the difference in temperatures between the upper and lower levels of ocean waters.

521. An oil-retrieving device to mop up oil from the surface of sea to curb marine pollution.

522. Clouds of foam made by detergents which contribute to water pollution.

523. An oil-skimmer for the emergency treatment of oil spills in harbours and in shore areas.

524. Those dots are the remnants of rockets, spacecraft, satellites, etc, which are surrounding the earth and creating what is called 'Space junk'. This is a computerised picture.

525. It is a solar energy house at Kapur Farms near New Delhi in which all energy for its functioning is supplied by solar energy.

SCORE YOURSELF!

Count the correct answers you have given
and mark
yourself as follows:

Average: if 450-474 answers are correct.

Good: if 475-499 answers are correct.

Excellent: if 500-524 answers are correct.

If you score more than 475, you are a
SUPER EXPERT in environment.